the Dessert Diaries

Gabi and the GREAT BIG Bakeover

by Laura Dower

STONE ARCH BOOKS
a capstone imprint

The Dessert Diaries is published by Stone Arch Books,
A Capstone Imprint
1710 Roe Crest Drive
North Mankato, Minnesota 56003

Library of Congress Cataloging-in-Publication Data is available on
the Library of Congress website.
978-1-4965-3119-3 (hardcover)
978-1-4965-4139-0 (paperback)
978-1-4965-3123-0 (eBook PDF)
Summary: Gabi is a sixth grader with a peanut allergy, artistic
talent, a bad case of shyness, and a first crush. A local baker with a
magical touch helps Gabi come out of her shell and use her talents
to help save her school.

Thanks to the Snack Patrol,
Myles, Livi, and Nate,
for their sweet (and smart) ideas —L.D.

Illustrated by Lilly Lazuli

Printed and bound in Canada.
009644F16

Table of Contents

It's Always Warm at Daisy's!

Home

Meet the Bakers

Recipes
- Cakes
- Cookies
- Tray Bakes
- Breads
- Gluten Free
- Vegan
- Dairy Free
- Other

Archive
- January
- February
- March

Hello, Sweeties!

So many surprises in store for the winter season! We have been open several months now, and I continue to get requests from all kinds of customers. Thank you for your feedback. Whenever someone asks me something in the bakery, I want you to know I am listening! You wanted bread! You wanted Kosher! We delivered!

My team (Carlos, Dina, Babs, and yours truly) is here to make you smile with all the sweet you can eat. Just give us a nudge if something doesn't work—or if there's something you wish we'd offer in the bakery. That's how we started up our pet snack section—because of customer requests (and some barking). Now we sell hundreds of doggy bone biscuits, and we are working on some treats for other pets too. There's always some delicious new idea in development at Daisy's.

Just speak up and tell us what *you* need, because it's *you* we're here for, after all!

Until we "sweet" again!

xo, Daisy

Chapter 1

That's Crummy

Gabriela shifted in her seat inside the school assembly. Kids to her left were elbowing each other—with the occasional bump into Gabi's side, which was beyond annoying. The kids on the right were sneaking peeks at their cell phones, which was not allowed—ever. It was very likely that at any moment, one of the teaching aides would bust the entire row and start to confiscate things. It was always like this at school these days: trouble-makers and fate-tempters surrounding Gabi, while she sat wishing she were invisible. Usually she *was* invisible. She was an outsider, even when she was in the middle of it all.

Gabi thought of the new book they'd been assigned in advanced language arts class, *The Outsiders* by S.E. Hinton. Gabi's pal Genna had read it before and said that it was "intense but in a good way," so Gabi was intrigued. Of course, Genna said most things were "intense": teachers, movies, songs, even Gabi's knee-high lace-up boots.

Gabi and Genna had been friends since kindergarten and called themselves G-squared, even though they were different in a lot of ways. Genna read everything and always had a book in her hands. Gabi didn't mind reading, but what she always had in her hand was a notebook and pencil. She loved sketching the world around her. Genna was athletic, and Gabi was clumsy. And while Genna was tall, Gabi was definitely not. Today Gabi had arrived late and couldn't find Genna in the chaos. So Gabi was stuck sitting next to a group of seventh-grade girls she didn't know.

The Outsiders was a funny book to be reading now considering how Gabi felt about school life.

Gabi thought maybe it was meant to be. After all, this year she was the ultimate outsider in so many ways: too few friends, too unsure of herself, too uninterested in the social drama around her ... the list went on and on. And sometimes kids teased her for her nut allergy that left her breathless in the lunchroom or covered in a red rash out of nowhere. Nobody wants attention for turning red and wheezing just from smelling someone's peanut butter sandwich. *Not* a lot of fun. Other kids with allergies didn't seem to get teased, but there was something about Gabi that just seemed ... teasable.

The reasons never really made sense.

Thankfully, during times like this, a pencil and a blank piece of paper were usually all Gabi needed to escape from the daily frustrations. Art got Gabi through most things, even tiresome assemblies like this one.

Art was like frosting on a cupcake that transformed the ordinary into something beautiful. Not that Gabi was allowed to *eat* cupcakes. In addition to possibly being contaminated with nuts, most baked goods were off limits because her mom insisted she eat gluten free as much as possible. "It's for our health, Gabi!" was her mom's constant refrain.

But still, a girl could dream. Like when her step-dad, Leo, gave her *Charlie and the Chocolate Factory* a few weeks earlier, Gabi filled half a sketchbook with Willy Wonka-inspired art, including Everlasting Gobstoppers and melting chocolate palaces from the story. Gabi also sketched regular life around her, including kids in the hallway or on the playing fields or even in assembly, like right now. She was way better with pictures than with words—especially spoken words.

Pictures helped Gabi make sense out of some of the nonsense surrounding her.

Up on stage the principal tapped on the micro-phone, and kids around Gabi settled into their seats and stashed away their phones. Well, some of them did. The girl right next to Gabi kept checking her photo app and taking selfies. Gabi rolled her eyes.

"Your attention, students," Principal Keystone said. "Eyes up here, please."

Gabi readied herself for a long, boring presentation. She slipped her sketchbook out of her bag and placed it flat on her lap. She tried to ignore the whispering, giggling girls around her and finish up a sketch of the stage. This was a challenging perspective, looking through the space between two kids' heads in front of her.

She sketched quickly, tuning out the giggling selfie girl in the seat next to hers. But then the girl elbowed Gabi hard in the ribs, causing her pencil to lurch and tear her paper.

"Hey!" Gabi gasped. Too loudly, she realized too late.

"What's your problem?" the girl snapped.

"I was drawing," Gabi said through her clenched teeth.

"Sheesh! Sorry. Don't freak out."

Gabi looked down at her ruined drawing and sighed. She was tongue-tied, as usual.

Ms. Munn, a teacher's aide standing at the end of the row, shot a glare at Gabi.

The gigglers giggled some more.

Ms. Munn crooked her finger and beckoned Gabi. "You, in the purple sweater, come with me."

Gabi was dumbfounded. She hadn't done anything! She glanced down to the end of the row, bristling at the giggling girls.

Ms. Munn put her hands on her hips and raised her eyebrows at Gabi. With a sigh, Gabi climbed over the row of girls with their book bags and wiggly knees and sneakers, trying hard not to trip and fall on her face. Nobody seemed to make any effort to get out of her way. The heavy satchel Gabi had slung over one shoulder combined with one girl's foot that stuck out at just the wrong time made Gabi lose her balance. She went flying, sprawling across people's laps. She bit her lip so as not to cry and got herself to the aisle where the aide was waiting.

"You're making a scene, young lady," Ms. Munn said.

"It wasn't me—" Gabi started to speak, but Ms. Munn shushed her.

Gabi clenched her jaw even tighter.

Up on stage, music was playing, slides were flashing, and Principal Keystone kept talking. Selfie Girl and her friends were looking innocently up at the stage, as if Principal Keystone was the most fascinating speaker ever. Gabi shook her head at their good-girl act.

"We cannot tolerate outbursts like that in assembly. Sit over here," Ms. Munn whispered in Gabi's face with toxic coffee breath. She directed Gabi to a row on the opposite side of the aisle, next to a boy Gabi had never seen before.

Gabi wanted to melt into the carpet. She was probably the least dramatic girl in the entire sixth grade, and yet she had been swept up into drama. She wanted nothing to do with it, but she didn't seem to have a choice. She huffed and sat down. Gabi felt the heat inside of her head ready to steam out her ears.

When Gabi looked back, she saw that Selfie Girl was now applying lip gloss. Huh? Wasn't there a rule about doing *that* in an assembly? Why wasn't Ms. Munn yelling at *her*? Different rules for different people.

Gabi located Genna in the crowd. Genna had clearly been trying to catch her eye. She shrugged as if to say, "What *was* that? Are you okay?"

Gabi mouthed so Genna could read her lips. "So unfair!"

The strange boy leaned over. "Did you say something?"

"What?" Gabi said in surprise.

The boy gave her a funny look then smiled.

Who was this? He had a tousle of dark hair, and deep dimples appeared in both cheeks when he talked. He had faded jeans on his long legs that barely seemed to fit in the row of seats. Gabi considered him like she'd consider a specimen in science class. And why did he smell so good, like the lime aftershave in the bathroom that her stepdad used?

He looked right into Gabi's eyes. "I guess assemblies stink at all schools, don't they?"

Gabi looked away. His eyes were too green. *Movie-star* green.

Principal Keystone was talking more loudly into the mic now, clearly getting excited about something. He launched into a lecture about test scores and test preparation. Gabi exhaled loudly, without even realizing she'd done it.

The boy leaned over to whisper again. "Is the principal always like this?"

Gabi allowed a small smile. "Always."

"I'm Max," the boy said.

Gabi nodded. "Hi, Max."

"Uh, do you have a name?"

"Oh," Gabi blushed. "Gabriela. Gabi for short. And I know, *I'm* short ..."

"Not that short. Unless you're actually standing up right now?" Max teased.

Gabi laughed. "So what's your story?" she asked, surprised by her own boldness.

Max smirked. "Well, I could tell you. But then I would have to kill you."

Gabi smiled again and shifted down into her seat. Out of the corner of her eye she caught Selfie Girl staring.

The microphone squealed loudly as Principal Keystone moved across the stage, gesturing wildly. Everyone clamped their hands to their ears at the sharp noise. A PowerPoint presentation was still running on the large screen behind him, slides flashing with words like "Energy" and "Students" and "Together!" This was the world's lamest pep talk.

"I'm in sixth. Are you?" Max whispered.

"Yup. And you?"

Max grinned again. "I just said that. I'm in sixth."

Gabi looked away. "Right."

"So what happened?" Max asked. "Why did you have to move seats?"

"It's a conspiracy," Gabi said, trying to make a joke.

"Sounds serious," Max said.

"Didn't you hear me yell?" Gabi asked.

"Nope. All I can hear is *him*. It's like the *Principal Keystone Show* up there."

Principal Keystone *was* shouting excitedly. He tapped the mic and it squealed again, louder this time. Everyone jeered and gasped at the piercing feedback noise.

Principal Keystone got back on track. "I want to boost our school pride and positive attitudes, and I know you have good ideas for us. Am I right?"

No one replied.

"AM I RIGHT?" Principal Keystone said again.

"YOUUUU'RE RIGHT!" one kid howled, sounding like the Tony the Tiger shouting, "They'rrre GREAT!"

There were muffled snickers. Then the worst possible thing happened: someone passed gas. Loudly. That's when the room went into hysterics.

Max mumbled, "Forget what I said. This assembly is way better than my old school's."

Gabi grinned. Max was nice. *And funny*.

Although she was laughing along with Max and everyone else, Gabi was also thinking. What Principal Keystone had said about school spirit and positivity caught her attention. She had some definite ideas about that. She was tired of all the mean attitudes and snarky comments that so many kids seemed to think were cool. The usual school-spirit tricks weren't working. T-shirt Spirit Day was a great big dud. Pep rallies were poorly attended. Kindness Day was an epic failure.

Gabi and Genna had often talked about how much better school would be if they had an art and photography club or a writing club or maybe even an art show or arts magazine. Something for students to work on together, a creative outlet to put their artistic skills to good use—instead of just being used to come up with colorful insults all the time.

Gabi had long dreamed of painting a fabulous mural in the shabby old school lobby. There was one wide wall there just begging for some school spirit to be painted all over it. Her brain was always abuzz with some new brainstorm, but she'd never been good at putting her ideas out into the universe. Instead, she'd just scribble them into her sketchbooks, hidden away from the world.

"So now that we know what we need, how do we do it?" Principal Keystone bellowed. "We need you students to help make our school even better! And in addition to school activities, we'll be inviting motivational speakers, authors, and people from our community to come share their stories. Think about what gets you excited and inspired. We will be hosting a student meeting Friday in the library during lunch for any who want to attend. So bring your ideas, and we'll see you there!"

The auditorium burst into clapping and a chorus of woots. Gabi felt an overwhelming urge to woot too, even though she suspected most of the other students were still cheering over the noisy fart and not Principal Keystone's idea. But everything Principal Keystone said had sounded good to Gabi.

The class bell rang.

"Please stay in order as you exit the auditorium, students!" Principal Keystone shouted over the roar of the crowd. Kids began standing and rushing into the aisles anyway.

"What homeroom are you?" Max asked as they made their way out of the row.

"Mr. Pollack's." Gabi had to shout to be heard over the screams and laughs of other students.

"Okay, well ... see you at that school-spirit meeting maybe?" Max asked.

"Maybe." Gabi smiled awkwardly. "Thanks for being nice," she said quickly. She rushed past him to join up with Genna and turned back to look at him. The funny thing was that he also turned back to look at her.

Awkward. And why had she thanked him for being nice? What a weird thing to say!

"Who is that?" Genna asked, racing to join her friend.

"Max," Gabi said coyly. "I guess he's new."

"I'm going to find out everything about him!" Genna joked.

"Genna!" Gabi groaned. "You're ridiculous."

"Boys are ridiculous," Genna said. "But I see it as my personal duty to investigate their strange species."

Gabi slugged her friend and laughed. "So did you hear what Principal Keystone said?" Gabi asked.

"Of course not," Genna said. "I was reading."

"He wants ideas for ways to increase school spirit," Gabi said. "What we've been talking about."

"Like art club?" Genna asked.

"Yes! Or my big mural idea. What's more spirited than a painting created by all the students together?"

"Totally! It's the best idea *ever*. We could even make it book themed! You should suggest it at the meeting ..." Genna said.

Gabi bit her lip. That was the part she wasn't sure about.

"Gabi! All the brilliant stuff in your notebooks

isn't going to change the world until you let other people see it!"

"Yeah, well ..." Gabi wrinkled her nose.

"You have all these great ideas, but you don't make them happen. They just sit there in your brain. I think that's why I am your friend. It's my job to help you put all of your good ideas into action. It'll be my mission in life!" she joked. "Besides investigating the male species, of course." She threw her arm around Gabi's shoulder and squeezed.

Gabi laughed as she wriggled out of Genna's boa constrictor grip. "We're late. Let's go."

Together they raced out of the assembly room, up two flights, and into their classroom. It was the middle of second period, advanced language arts, and the teacher decided to give everyone a pop quiz.

Not surprisingly, the entire class was completely freaking out.

Because Gabi and Genna were in the advanced class, they were lucky enough (not) to be in with lots of seventh graders. Selfie Girl and a couple of her friends from assembly were just a few desks away, watching Gabi—probably to see if she was going to trip again, Gabi thought. Gabi did her best to ignore them, but every time one of them giggled or whispered, Gabi couldn't help but think that it was somehow related to her.

Before the quiz got started, Genna scribbled a note and slid it across the floor to Gabi.

Ignore the idiots

Gabi smiled and scribbled back:

Actively ignoring ☺

Genna resumed with the notes right after the quiz ended.

Let's walk home today—SECRET plan

Both girls lived only a few blocks from school and around the corner from each other. When the three o'clock bell rang, the pair rendezvoused by the front doors of the school. The crowds were all pushing out onto the street like a tidal wave.

Genna nearly collided with Gabi as they squeezed out of the building. She produced a baggie filled with crumbly little cookies. "Coconut snaps! Want one?"

"Genna, you know I can't have nuts."

"*Coconut* isn't a nut!" Genna laughed out loud.

"I know that! But still, I think I'm going to skip it, just in case," Gabi said. "You know my worrywart mom. No cookies for me."

Genna shrugged and asked, "Have you seen that new bakery that opened near us?"

"You mean Daisy's Desserts? Yeah, I saw their grand opening awhile back. TV cameras everywhere. So cool. I didn't go inside, cuz of the peanut thing and all that, but it's right across from my apartment building."

"Oh, you've got to see the inside! It's like a movie set with painted tables and mismatched chairs. And there's these funky waitresses, and this tattooed muscle man. Oh! And a baker with wild red hair flying all over the place," Genna said, breathlessly. "I went with Mom and we pigged out on cinnamon buns and these ummy-yummy apple squares and we took a bunch more to-go. Mom said the whole place is sprinkled in fairy dust."

"And peanut dust, probably," Gabi muttered. "I can see it from my bedroom window. I like how it has those little white lights. It *does* look magical."

"Let's stop on the way home!" Genna suggested. "You don't have to eat anything. We can just look."

"You mean *I* can just look ... while you grab like fifty cakes and snarf them? No thanks!" Gabi was always amazed at her friend's bottomless stomach.

"Hey, that's a crummy thing to say!" Genna cried, and then she laughed at her own joke. "Get it? Crummy?"

"Hilarious," Gabi sighed. "*A bakery joke?* That is really half-baked, Gen."

"Ha! Half-baked! Now I've got you doing it too!"

Gabi stuck her tongue out sideways and made a goofy face. "You know I can't go anywhere until we finish homework," she said. "And you know my mom expects me to come straight home."

"Well, then I guess we're doing homework first,"

Genna replied. "But let's hurry, cuz homework makes me hungry!"

The pair took off down the street toward Gabi's building, winter coats flying loose behind them on the balmy winter day.

Chapter 2

Home Sweet Home

Priority number one: do math homework. But Genna decided somewhere between word problems five and six that she'd much rather watch TV or paint nails or especially venture across the street to the new bakery. She was very persistent. But Gabi stayed strong and insisted they get their work done first.

Gabi's bedroom walls were covered with art, of course: paintings, ink drawings, and pencil sketches that she had done over the years. "When did you do this?" Genna asked, pointing to a series of smaller sketches that Gabi had framed together. It showed the progression of a tree losing its leaves, little by little. "You are so talented Gabi. You could totally be president of Art Club."

"If we *had* an art club," Gabi said.

Genna flitted around the bedroom, picking up scarves and poking her fingers into baskets of jewelry and hair ties. She modeled one of Gabi's sweaters—a cable-knit, over-sized golden wool one with chunky wooden buttons.

"Where did you get this?" Genna asked.

Gabi shrugged. "You know my mom. Thrift-shop bargain."

"She's too cool," Genna sighed.

"Shopping second hand is *not* always cool, especially when you're doing it to save money," Gabi said.

"But it can be cool if someone has as much style as you," Genna said, holding up a blue cardigan with a leather belt. "I love all your big funky sweaters!"

Gabi gave a small twist of a smile. "It is fun, mixing and matching," she admitted. She liked adding infinity scarves and wearing different camisole tanks and patterned leggings. "I'm really into necklaces now too. Leo says I'm going to be a fashion designer. He just bought me a case of new sketchbooks. Have I showed them to you?"

Genna laughed. "What do you have, like two-hundred by now?"

All along the side of Gabi's room were bookshelves lined with thin black books. In silver Sharpie marker on the spines of each were dates and simple labels like "Art," "Fairies," "Fashionista," "Vacation," "Family," "Desserts," "Fish," and dozens more. All of her favorite topics had sketchbooks devoted to them. They went as far back as first grade, as far back as Leo joining the family. Leo was quite possibly the best stepfather in the entire world. He got her more than anyone ever had.

"I wanna try on some more of your stuff," Genna declared. She grabbed armfuls from Gabi's closet and modeled some of the hats and sweaters, dramatically posing in the mirror with each new ensemble. Gabi turned up the radio and they shook and twisted to the funky beats.

The large picture window in Gabi's room was covered up with curtains that Gabi had sewn with her *abuela*. They were a beautiful yellow flowered pattern. Out of breath from dancing, Genna tugged them open and stared down onto the city street.

"You weren't kidding! Daisy's Desserts is right there, and you can see *everything*," Genna said. "Couldn't we have just peeked inside before we came up here? I could really, really, *really* use a cookie."

"Let's have some carrots and hummus instead," Gabi said. "And we came up here first because of my mom's rule, remember? That's how she rolls. I can't 'just stop quickly' *anywhere*. She's watching the clock from the moment the dismissal bell rings at school."

"Sometimes it's hard being best friends with a rule-follower like you."

"I think we might have some cookies in the

kitchen," Gabi said, ignoring her comment. "They taste like cardboard, though. The gluten-free and nut-free ones my mom buys are kind of gross. But you can try them."

Genna made a "blech" face. "Sounds tempting," she said sarcastically.

All at once, Gabi's mom swept into the bedroom with an overflowing laundry basket.

"Grabriela!" she cried out, looking around at the stuff all over the floor. "*Lo que es un lío!*"

"Mamá," Gabi whined. "My room is NOT a mess!"

Genna bounced on the edge of the bed. "Hey, Señora Rivera."

"Hola, Genna. What's up?"

"The sky, hot-air balloons, birds," Genna said, falling back dramatically onto the pillows.

Gabi's mom laughed. "Are you still taking Spanish class?"

Genna shrugged. "I stink at Spanish. No offense."

"You just need more practice!" Gabi's mom said. "You girls expect everything to come so easily."

She looked down at the load of wash in her arms. "I have to go throw this into the machine downstairs. Did you girls get a snack? We have veggies ..."

"Wait! We can help," Genna piped up. "We can take the laundry downstairs. And we can do our homework in the laundry room while we wait to put it in the dryer. Right, Gabs?"

Gabi looked at Genna like she was crazy. Why was she volunteering their entire afternoon to help with chores?

"Great!" Gabi's mom said, thrilled with the offer. She dropped the laundry basket onto the floor. Some shirts spilled out. "Let me get you the detergent," she said.

"Mamá—" Gabi started to protest, but she had disappeared down the hall.

"Genna, why did you volunteer us?" Gabi whined.

"Don't you see? If we go downstairs, we can sneak across the street!" Genna whispered, tilting her head toward the window.

A light bulb went off over Gabi's head. Of course. Daisy's Desserts. Genna was persistent all right.

"You are still obsessing about your cookies?" Gabi hesitated, then said, "Okay fine, we'll do it. But I still have to get my homework done." She reached into her kitty-cat ceramic bank and grabbed a few dollar bills. "You are a real nag."

Genna nodded proudly.

Ten minutes later, the girls were filling a washing machine with darks and putting in extra quarters for the gentle cycle. Then they headed up a set of back stairs and raced through the building lobby, Genna leading the way, of course. She had built-in radar for cookies, after all.

"So, I set my phone timer," Gabi said. "It'll beep when we need to come back and throw the clothes into the dryer."

"I can't believe I actually talked you into this!" Genna squealed as they headed out the door and across the street, looking both ways for traffic.

"This is going to be un-fun," Gabi said with a sigh.

"I hate bakeries because I can't ever eat any of the stuff." She looked around to make sure Leo or one of her mom's friends weren't around to rat on them.

"This place may be different. You'll see."

"Doubt it."

"Well, I can eat it and describe it to you in detail," Genna said, smirking. "And how can you not love this place? Look at the sign: *Baked Love.*"

Festive holiday decorations hung all over the bakery windows. Snowy frost letters spelled out *Come inside and get toasty!* across the width of the window. Lights and ribbons were strung everywhere, making the place look like a winter fairyland.

"Wow!" Gabi said, pressing her nose to the glass. People were crowded in at the various painted tables, sipping from large mugs of coffee and eating sweet treats. "You were right. It *is* like a movie." Everyone inside looked like an actor paid to act like they were having the time of their lives—the best cookies, the best coffee, the best conversations, the best company. But they were real people.

They stepped inside.

"Welcome!" called out a woman with a beautiful gray and black braid twisted over one shoulder. Gabi squinted to read her nametag: DINA. Another woman, who looked like a movie star from another generation, waved and called out "Howdy girlies!" Her tag read BABS, and she wore bright red lipstick and her silver hair in a poufy beehive.

Gabi and Genna waved shyly at the bakers then looked at each other and giggled.

Wonderful smells overwhelmed Gabi's senses. It smelled so good that she couldn't help inhaling deeply, even though she was afraid there might be peanut dust in the air. But all she smelled was chocolate and vanilla and lemon and blueberry. Yum. If only she could try something—*anything*! But she thought back to the last scary allergy attack she'd had in fourth grade and reminded herself that she could never let her guard down. She was just here for Genna to get something, and then they'd have to leave.

Dina found Gabi and Genna a small table near the back counter. There was a cup of crayons on the table, probably for busy little toddlers, but Gabi grabbed a fistful of blues and golds and reds. She began to draw on the paper covering the table while Genna went to browse the glass display cabinet of goodies. When in doubt, draw. That was her rule. Gabi turned all of her frustration at not being able to stuff her face with cookies like Genna could into creative energy.

Gabi focused on her artwork. She drew all the different pastries and pies from the shop that she could see: cupcakes with whipped peaks of pink frosting; chocolate cakes with layer upon layer of fudgy goodness; and monster cookies as big as her face with a million different ingredients thrown in.

Gabi giggled to think that the cookie really *would* be a monster if she ate it, since it most likely contained nuts. She drew furry arms and legs coming out of the cookie and made a silly face with sharp fangs in the middle of it. Now it really was a "monster cookie."

"Hey, do you mind if I eat this?" Genna asked, appearing at her side. She held up a chocolate chip cookie measuring six inches around.

Gabi pulled away from it and wrinkled her nose, but she shook her head and went back to her artwork. "Just keep your crumbs to yourself."

"GABS!" Genna grabbed Gabi's arm so hard that a jagged crayon line appeared over her monster drawing. Twice in one day!

"Hey! Why did you do that?" Gabi asked. "You ruined my monster cookie monster!"

Then Gabi looked in the direction that Genna was subtly pointing.

It was him. The new kid, Max, was there. He'd come in with a crew from school, even some kids from the grade above. *That was fast*, Gabi thought. It didn't take long for him to settle in with all the cool kids ... including Selfie Girl and her entourage.

Gabi wondered why she felt so excited to run

into Max again. What would she say to him—if they even talked at all? As usual, Gabi was awfully good at wondering—and not so good at saying much of anything.

"OMG, I think he's coming over," Genna whispered, poking Gabi again.

And indeed he was. Making a beeline, in fact.

"Hey, it's you," Max said, smiling. "Gabriela."

"I guess he remembers you," Genna mumbled so only Gabi could hear.

Gabi kicked Genna under the table but kept her face turned up to Max.

"Hey, it's you too," she said, trying to hide her nerves. "What's up? Come with friends?"

"I came with those guys," he said, nodding to the group. "I don't know the girls. My neighbor, Pablo, hangs with them. We live around the corner, in that building with the crane out front."

"What a coincidence," Genna blurted. "Gabi lives right across the street, actually. So you're neighbors, destined to meet—"

Gabi quickly placed a flat palm over Genna's mouth. "Aren't we all neighbors?" Gabi said, pretending like her BFF had *not* just said what she said.

"Okay, well, I'm going to get one of those apple bars. My mom bought some last week, and they are really good. You should try them."

"Mmm," Gabi hummed, completely out of things to say.

Awkward again.

Max glanced down at the table and spotted Gabi's artwork. "Whoa. Did you draw that? You're really good."

"She's like some kind of artistic genius, right?" Genna said.

Gabi rolled her eyes. Thankfully, Dina swept over to the table just then and set a cup of tea next to Gabi's space. She placed a jar of honey there with a few napkins. "Will you be joining these lovely ladies?" she asked Max.

Max shook his head nervously. "Uhh …"

"You better get back to your other friends," Gabi

said, trying to let him off the hook. "And get that apple bar."

"Or maybe I should get a big cookie like yours," Max said to Genna. "Aren't you getting anything, Gabi?"

"No cookies. I'm allergic."

"Oh, bummer." Max said.

"Yup, to tree nuts and peanuts anyway. And my mom makes us avoid gluten. Basically, I can eat lettuce and that's it. Ha! Just kidding. Sort of ..."

Max looked at her with a blank stare.

Gabi was embarrassed that she had rambled on about her dumb food issues. "Um," she said, "your friends are leaving."

Gabi saw that the group Max had come with was heading for the door. "See you in school, then?" he asked.

Gabi wanted to touch those deep dimples that appeared whenever he smiled. He waved goodbye and went to the counter to get his cookie. Gabi noticed one or two of the girls in the group, but they didn't see her. Or at least they pretended not to, thank goodness.

Genna crossed her arms and cocked her head to one side.

"Hold on. Did I miss something?" Genna looked confused. "He is so normal."

"No major flaws is good, right?" Gabi said.

"Gabs, he had on a Wave Rider shirt," Genna said. "He obviously listens to cool music. This is all very good news."

"I guess, yeah," Gabi said and shrugged. "But all it means is he'll figure out soon that I'm *not* the cool-enough person he should be talking to. When he finds out what those girls in his new posse think of me, he won't be so friendly."

"What?" Genna threw her arms into the air with exasperation. "Stop saying that stuff. You're always talking about yourself like you're some lame girl. Quit the pity party, my friend. You have style. You have talent. And I know what I am talking about."

Gabi sighed. "I know. Sometimes I just can be so—"

"Annoying?" Genna groaned.

"Well, the word I was looking for was *insecure,* but okay I guess I'm apparently annoying too ..."

Genna just shrugged and took a big bite of her cookie.

"Thanks, *amiga,*" Gabi said and stuck out her tongue playfully.

"You know I'm here to help," Genna replied, matter-of-fact.

Gabi took her black crayon and scribbled on top of the art she'd drawn before. She pressed down hard with zigzags.

"What did you do that for?" Genna cried.

"Better than yelling at you, right?" Gabi said, arching one eyebrow.

"No fighting please," Genna said. "I'm sorry. Sometimes—I just wish you weren't so hard on yourself. You know?"

"Got it," Gabi said with a sheepish smile. She

sipped her hot tea, pouring in more honey and squeezing a pinch of lemon juice until it tasted just right. The tea was spearmint and chamomile, warm and comforting, just like the tea Leo made.

"Hello, gals! Is everything all right?"

Suddenly a smiling woman was standing in front of their table, hands on her hips and crazy red hair trying to escape from the flowered scarf on her head.

"You're Daisy!" Genna said as if she were meeting a celebrity. Genna held up her now-half-eaten cookie, as if to say, "You're the magician who made this!"

"I am indeed!" Daisy gave her a big thumbs-up. "Mega Cookie! Good choice. Are you ladies good with your treats?" She looked down at Gabi's lonely cup of tea without pastry accompaniment.

"No cakes for you?" Daisy asked, eyebrows raised. "Highly unusual. And what's with the cookie monster?" She laughed and pointed at Gabi's half-scribbled out monster cookie artwork.

"Highly allergic." Genna did the explaining for Gabi.

"Really?" Daisy gave her a surprised look. "What timing! Just this week I was making some plans to start offering some nut-free, gluten-free, and dairy-free items."

"Really?" Gabi's eyes lit up. "That is a crazy coincidence."

Daisy winked. "Maybe! But some things are meant to be." She sat and talked with the girls for several minutes, asking Gabi about her allergies and what types of allergy-free treats she'd most like to have. Daisy told her that they were planning to add some protected areas in her kitchen that would be safe food-prep counters for certain allergens, all with their own equipment.

Gabi was shocked that Daisy was taking time out of her day to ask about Gabi's "special needs." She hated having the attention on herself, but on the other hand, she was thrilled that Daisy seemed to truly care.

In fact, Daisy even thanked Gabi for talking with her. "It's so nice to have an expert consultant to talk to!" Daisy said. "It's almost like fate brought you in here today, just as I am making some decisions about allergy-friendly recipes. I want my bakery to be for everyone—including you!" Daisy touched Gabi's shoulder and headed back to the kitchen, tucking stray curls back into her scarf as she went.

Gabi turned to look at Genna. "Can you believe that?" she asked.

Just then, Gabi's phone beeped loudly, making the girls jump. It sounded like an alien spaceship.

"That's our laundry deadline!" Gabi said.

Genna inhaled the last three bites of her cookie and chewed madly.

"Hurry! My mom will check up on us. If she goes down to the laundry room and we aren't there, she'll ..."

"Fwwwweak!" Genna said through the last mouthful of her Mega-Cookie.

They grabbed their stuff and headed out the

door of the bakery. Gabi looked behind them for Daisy, but she didn't see her to say goodbye.

They raced back across the street and into the apartment lobby, zipping down the stairs, all the way back to the laundry room.

And there was Gabi's mom, standing there in the doorway, arms crossed.

The two friends locked hands and froze as they skidded to a stop. There was nothing to say. They'd been caught.

"Gabriela Rivera, where were you?" Gabi's mom asked sternly. "And don't think you're not in trouble too, Genna Wells!"

The girls gulped.

"We went for a walk," Gabi said. "And I set my phone timer ..."

All at once the phone beeped again, even louder this time, the sounds pinging off the cement walls.

"Time to put the clothes in the dryer ..." Genna said weakly.

"You set a timer?" Gabi's mom said, surprised.

"We were being responsible, Mamá," Gabi said. "I swear."

Mom took a deep breath. "So where were you?"

Gabi looked sideways at Genna and saw a smear of chocolate on her face. They were busted.

"Um ... the bakery across the street?" Gabi confessed.

"Bakery! What were you thinking! You may as well have gone into a war zone! Gabi, you know better. That is too dangerous for you!"

"But Señora Rivera, she didn't even eat anything. She only drank boring old tea!" Genna said.

Gabi's mom shook her head. Her forehead was crinkled with worry. "Gabi, you remember what happened in fourth grade, right? You can't take these risks."

"Mamá, how could I forget? You'll never *let* me! I am *always* careful. The peanuts aren't going to come after me. I am smart—you know that."

Gabi's mom sighed. "We'll discuss later. For now, back upstairs with you to finish your work.

Next time, girls, *ask* me before you go running off and abandoning a load of laundry. I'll finish things up down here. You need to wash up anyway, right Genna?" She turned on her heel and went back into the laundry room.

"Yikes," Genna said. "And what's the matter with my face? Why was your mom looking at it?"

"You have chocolate all over it!" Gabi told her.

"Oops," Genna said and then broke out in a grin. She tried to lick the corners of her mouth to get the extra chocolate. "Well, the Mega Cookie was totally worth it, no matter what happens!"

Chapter 3

Peppermint Dust

Not even a full day went by before Gabi found herself heading back to the bakeshop. As much as she wanted to smell those delicious sweets again, what she really wanted was to see Daisy. There was something about her that gave Gabi hope.

The night before, as Gabi's mom and Leo were talking after dinner, Gabi had gotten up the courage to ask if she could stop at Daisy's on her way home from school the next afternoon. Gabi's mom bit her lip for a moment and looked at Leo. Finally, she said a very surprising "Okay, but be careful." Leo winked at Gabi.

Gabi had told her mom about Daisy and all the questions she had asked about her allergies. Maybe that was why she gave Gabi permission to go there. It seemed that this baker named Daisy was taking Gabi's allergy seriously, which not everyone did. Like the time of her last attack in fourth grade, when a waitress promised them their food wasn't fried in peanut oil ... and it was. Gabi had gone into anaphylactic shock (translation: the worst possible kind of stop-breathing allergic reaction), and her throat start to close up. It had been terrifying. Leo had had to administer Gabi's EpiPen. Luckily, it saved Gabi and made it so she could breathe again, but she'd still had to go to the ER to be checked out.

Since then Gabi's mom didn't seem to trust *anybody* when it came to feeding her daughter. She exemplified the term worrywart.

So what had changed now?

Gabi didn't want to think too hard or too long about it. She wouldn't question Mom's response— she'd just go. Solo. Freedom!

Walking inside the bakery, the smells hit her again, but there were different ones now. Cinnamon maybe? And cherry? She took a seat at another paper-covered wooden table that leaned to one side and was propped under one leg with little sugar packets to stop it from wobbling. Around the café, Gabi spotted a few other kids from school, ignoring her as always. There was also a table of old men yelling over each other about politics.

Gabi watched as Daisy swooped in on the table where the men sat, bringing new sweets to eat. Magically, Daisy's cheery smile and plate of sweets made the old guys quiet down, as if she was putting them into some kind of trance. She appeared to have an unknowable, un-seeable power over people and things inside her bakery.

Daisy was the opposite of invisible, like Gabi felt. She watched Daisy with her customers and staff and saw that Daisy's presence was undeniably *visible*, and it affected other people in a good way. Whether she was helping a customer choose the best cupcakes for a party or showing one of the other bakers where to put the pie display, she seemed … valuable. Like what she had to say mattered.

It hit Gabi like a palm to the forehead that she wanted to feel like that too—to share her ideas with other people and be heard.

Gabi inhaled deeply and clasped her hands in her lap, just watching the busy bakery hubbub. Even though she knew she couldn't eat the food, Gabi felt safe somehow, safer here than just about anywhere. Nobody rolling their eyes at her or teasing her. Just sitting there, watching and drawing, Gabi felt as satisfied as if she had eaten a real, whipped-cream-covered dessert.

Of course she couldn't spend all afternoon crowd watching. There was homework to be done. Gabi pulled out her books. Maybe she'd try one of the fancy hot chocolates while she studied her vocabulary. Nobody put nuts in those, she was pretty sure.

As Gabi was considering this, Daisy came over.

"We've got some rather ridiculous new hot beverages on our menu."

"I was just looking at those," Gabi said.

Daisy pointed to a chalkboard with a list of the day's offerings in fancy curlicue script. She also grabbed a menu designed with high glossy paper and brilliant photos of the items. There were coffees in all sizes and strengths, and iced teas in flavors like black licorice and raspberry. How could there possibly be this many drink options? Gabi saw three she picked out as the best:

Candy Crush
(hot steamed cocoa with cloud of whipped cream and peppermint candy dust)

Gimme S'More
(hot chocolate with toasted mini-marshmallows and crushed graham crackers)

Snickerdoodley
(cinnamon sugar drizzle over hot white cocoa with a caramel stirring stick)

Nearly drooling at the thought of these delicious options, Gabi finally settled on the peppermint dust. Peppermint dust sounded like *fairy* dust, which was of course magical! Maybe this place *did* have some kind of special power? Anything was possible.

When Daisy floated away to get the cocoa, Gabi opened her sketchbook and began to draw in that instead of on the table. She wanted to keep these sketches more private. Gabi felt inspired by the thought of candy dust—a whole cloud of it sweeping over the room—putting everyone into a candy trance.

Once she began to sketch, Gabi's mind went for a long, wild ramble as her pencil wandered all over the page. She was drawing fast and furious— whatever came to mind or whatever her eyes landed upon.

Gabi sketched the lady at the next table taking a bite of her quite-oversized cupcake and the jostling bunch of kids lining up to buy afterschool cookies to go. She began to daydream a little bit, flipping through the pages of the book that she had already filled with sketches of pies and cakes and whatever else was sold at the bakery. There were a few sketches of Genna making funny faces. And a few more of Max. Close-ups of his face. One was half-torn out of the book. Gabi considered ripping it out because, in a moment of bravery, she'd doodled something on the side:

I ♡ *Max*

It was always dangerous to confess your crush out loud, but even *more* dangerous to confess it on the pages of a book in permanent ink.

Daisy reappeared with an enormous mug of cocoa in her hand.

Gabi quickly shut her sketchbook and shoved it into her backpack already stuffed with books and binders. Sixth grade had been the introduction of back-breaking textbooks that needed to go home every single night.

"Here you go!" Daisy said, placing the steaming cup in front of Gabi. The whipped cream was thick but melting fast. There was more than just pink minty dust on top—Gabi could see little chips of candy cane too. Too good not to have a lick off the top. *Mint-a-licious!*

"So it's rough having allergies, huh?" Daisy asked.

Gabi shrugged and wiped the whipped cream mustache off her lip. "I'm used to it. I just have to explain it over and over. It's more *annoying* than rough."

"Have you ever had an attack? Eaten nuts by mistake?" Daisy asked.

"Yeah," Gabi said. She told Daisy about the restaurant, and about another incident at school when a new girl accidentally sat at the peanut-free table and Gabi's napkin had gotten too close to the girl's peanut butter sandwich. "The nurse had to give me my EpiPen. You know what that is, right? It gives you a dose of epinephrine, this emergency drug."

Daisy nodded. "You're very brave."

"Brave?" Gabi asked. "I think there are plenty of braver girls than me. I mean, I *wish* I was brave ..."

Gabi stopped mid-sentence. She had no idea why she was sharing any of this with Daisy, who she'd only met yesterday. And yet, she wanted to share. She wanted to be heard.

Daisy was leaning on her elbows now, real close, hanging on Gabi's every word.

"Well, the thing is, sometimes the kids at school, well ... they don't really get me."

"What do you mean?" Daisy asked, cocking her head sideways.

"I don't know," Gabi shrugged. "I'm an easy target because of my allergies and being short and kind of clumsy and the way I dress and ..."

Daisy frowned. "I hate to hear that, Gabi."

"I'm just not like other girls."

"And that's a bad thing?"

"You wouldn't understand," Gabi murmured.

"More than you know. This frizzy red mop brought me a lifetime of Brillo pad and clown-wig comments. It's like people feel entitled to make fun of something that's the slightest bit unique."

Gabi nodded knowingly.

"I tried my hardest to blend in, but I always ended up getting noticed," Daisy said with a laugh.

"I feel like I blend in *too* much—right into the background!" Gabi said. "Until someone notices something they want to make fun of, that is ..."

"But you know what? You can embrace what makes you different. I'll tell you what—I wouldn't trade my crazy red hair for anything now, even though as a kid I wore hats to try to hide it! And hon, your sense of style may not be appreciated by the middle schoolers you're surrounded by, but someday, I guarantee, people will be asking *you* for fashion advice." Daisy nodded emphatically and tugged the sleeve of Gabi's army-green plaid jacket.

Gabi grinned. "You know what? I think I'm a lot like my *abuela*. She sews all of her own clothes, and they're beautiful! And even though she's really short like me, she walks down the street just as proud as a peacock."

"And she should! What else does she say?"

"She says I am *hermosa* ... beautiful," Gabi said shyly.

"I think she's absolutely right. And it sounds like she cares a lot about you. I bet she's a good hugger too. My Nana Belle was the best hugger on the planet."

"Yeah, she is a great hugger," Gabi agreed. "But her hugs can't fix these dumb allergies." She twisted her lips into a half-frown. "I guess I'm just used to being on the outside looking in. It stinks to have to sit at the peanut-free lunch table. If that doesn't make me queen of the dorks, then what does?"

"Hey," Daisy said, "I thought I was the queen of the dorks!"

They laughed together.

"Listen, Gabi. No one has a right to make fun of you for *anything*. Remember that. Not your allergies. Not your height. *Nothing*. Take a hint from your abuela and walk tall. Okay? I think you've got more to offer the world than you're letting on. Be proud of yourself. Own your talents *and* your differences. Okay?"

"Thanks," Gabi said, and her mind flitted over the school-spirit meeting and her mural idea.

Daisy stood up. "Let me get you a refill on that cocoa."

"That would be great. Thank you," Gabi said, taking the last sip. There was still a bit of peppermint dust on the rim of the cup. "More fairy dust, please," she said with a giggle.

Daisy winked. "I have to check on something in the back, but I'll come with the refill in a jiff. Don't go anywhere."

As soon as Daisy wandered off, Gabi pulled out her sketchbook again. A stack of loose pages inside it started to slip out, and she juggled to keep any from falling on the floor. Her eyes landed on some pastries she had drawn. She could draw just about every pastry and cookie in this place. Maybe Daisy would like her pictures? Or maybe she wouldn't? She wanted to be brave enough to show her

GABI AND THE GREAT BIG BAKEOVER

artwork, but she didn't know how. "Walking tall" was easier said than done.

A burly, tattooed baker with a nametag that read CARLOS scooted around the bakery with a broom. He swept up leftover crumbs from all over and gathered cups and saucers that had been emptied and left on tables. He whistled a cheery tune as he worked, greeting other customers by name and joking with the gruff old men. When he pushed his broom past Gabi's table, he leaned over and looked at her artwork. "You got some kind of magic in those fingers?"

Gabi blushed and shook her head. "Just talent, I guess!" she said, remembering Daisy's advice to "own her talents." Starting now! Carlos nodded, impressed, and started whistling again as he swept his way back to the kitchen.

Gabi felt inspired. She began to sketch on a fresh sheet of paper. This time she drew Daisy with her beautiful bouquet of curly red hair, arms wide open, and a warm smile on her face. She sketched out large D-A-I-S-Y letters with flourishes and stars. Making very cool bubble letters on her sketches was part of the fun. She penciled in more details as quickly as she could.

There was a loud jingle-jangle at the bakery front door. Gabi lifted her head to see who had come in. A bunch of loud kids ambled inside. And there in the center of the group was Max, once again surrounded by other kids who Gabi recognized from the class above hers—including Selfie Girl.

Gabi abruptly slammed her sketchbook shut. Was there some magic way to turn invisible now? She worried that if anyone noticed her at all, they might say something mean, like "interesting outfit—garage-sale chic?" An older girl had said that to her before, and her face still burned from the memory.

Instead, nothing happened. No one looked at her. *Not even a sideways glance.* Gabi sighed. That's what she had wanted ... wasn't it?

"Here's your second helping of fairy-dust

cocoa!" announced Daisy, suddenly placing a cup in front of Gabi. But Gabi was so surprised that she startled, flinging her arm and sending the piping hot chocolate cup flying.

"*Nooooo!*"

There was steaming peppermint-whipped-cream mess on everything now.

"Oh, dear!" Daisy exclaimed.

Gabi's eyes went wide. Surely everyone was staring at her now.

"I'm sorry! I have to go!" Gabi blustered. "I mean, like right now. I'm so sorry." She slipped on her coat, trying to hide from her classmates beneath it.

Daisy looked confused.

Babs rushed over with a mop for the floor. The big group of kids took over a couple of tables, laughing and acting loud and silly. Gabi kept her head down so as not to meet anyone's eye.

"I'm so sorry—the peppermint mess is all my fault," Gabi said to Daisy as she slung her bag over one shoulder. But it was unzipped, and all those loose sketch papers flew everywhere. Gabi quickly grabbed them, shoving them crinkled and ripped back into her bag, and rushed out the door.

"You don't have to go!" Daisy called out.

But Gabi, mortified, was already running across the street to the safety of her apartment.

Chapter 4

A Baker's Dozen

After the bakery incident, Gabi declared that she would stay locked up in her apartment forever and only come out for classes and tests. Her mom would never let her skip school, though. The embarrassment from what had happened in the shop hung over her like a black rain cloud for days. She'd spilled the hot drink, dropped her sketchbook, and generally made a scene. There was no rebounding from *that*.

Enter: best friend who won't take no for an answer—and won't let someone throw a pity party, either. There was no use crying over spilled cocoa, Genna said.

She insisted that Gabi needed to do at least one thing this week, and that was to go with her to the school-spirit meeting. She had at least a dozen pretty good reasons, including: "You can't stay on the couch and watch TV forever," and "You owe me," and, most important, "This might be your one and only chance to do that art mural you've been dreaming about forever!"

"Wait. Go back. Did you say I *owe* you?" Gabi said, raising an eyebrow.

"Well, you know what I mean. I *need* you there. Same dif. And I'm serious about the TV. You can DVR everything and watch it later."

Gabi fake-punched Genna's shoulder and smiled. "You stink."

"I do not. I put on a bunch of that Rose Petal Power spray this morning after I took a shower!"

"Look, Genna, if I go, I am just there to support you," Gabi said. "Someone will probably tease me if I open my mouth, like they always do …"

"What is this 'always' business?" Genna said.

"No one is going to tease you. Frankly, I doubt the meanies will even show up. No one will even notice you're there."

"Gee, thanks," Gabi groaned.

"You can do this," Genna said. "We can do this."

"Okay, okay," Gabi said. She knew the truth: she had to participate in the school-spirit meeting and share her ideas. She had to get out of her rut. Genna was right ... and so was Daisy.

On Friday at noon, the meeting was called to order. At least forty students showed up. Gabi peeked around the room but didn't see Max. He must have changed his mind about coming. Gabi felt a small pang of disappointment but also relief. She didn't want to face him after what happened at Daisy's.

Principal Keystone launched into one of his usual "let's get fired up!" speeches. "Thank you, students, for coming. Let's create the change we want to see!" *Blah, blah, blah.*

A pair of eighth-grade students had come prepared with a list of ideas they had photocopied and distributed them to everyone.

School-Spirit Week

School-Spirit Day

School-Spirit Spelling Bee

School-Spirit Game Show

"Those are cool ideas!" Genna whispered.

Gabi rolled her eyes. "What ideas? These are just a bunch of random titles. What's the difference between School-Spirit Week and School-Spirit Day?"

"Six days?" Genna cracked, trying to be cute.

Gabi actually laughed out loud. She deserved that joke. She realized she needed to be more optimistic here. She was as bad as the meanies if she was going to trash everyone else's ideas.

One kid suggested hosting a carnival with games and prizes. But other kids thought that might be too babyish. The spelling bee idea sounded too academic. The game show was funny but complicated.

Genna nudged her. "Bring up your idea!" she hissed. But Gabi shook her head.

Everyone started talking over each other and interrupting. Mostly they were all talking about things that had nothing *whatsoever* to do with school spirit and positive attitudes.

"I heard about this thing they did at another school," some kid piped up. "It's called Treats for Tests. On exam days they'll give out Popsicles. Or granola bars. Something fun."

"Granola bars do not give me spirit," Genna whispered and made a funny face.

Voices murmured lukewarm responses to that idea. This wasn't exactly the most productive meeting ever held. Was anyone even taking notes on all this stuff?

Finally more ideas started rolling in, and Principal Keystone jotted them on the smart board.

Host a lip synch contest
Have a nerd day
Do a good deed daily
Schoolwide sports challenge

"I know. We could have twin day!" Genna suggested a few moments later. "Everyone in school would dress up like someone else—maybe someone famous. Your famous twin! That's something that's done during school-spirit week, right?"

Gabi thought that sounded cute, though possibly as unrelated to school spirit as granola. Principal Keystone scratched his head but wrote it on the board anyway.

"We can plant a tree," someone else said.

"We could paint the inside of the school building bright yellow like sunshine so everyone is happier," some kid from seventh grade said.

Someone snorted rudely. "Great idea, we'll all be blinded by the brightness."

It reminded Gabi of all the times anyone had ever teased her about her allergies or anything else. She had to say something.

"We could paint something else in the school," Gabi said, trying to speak loudly enough to be heard. "Together."

The snorting kid laughed again. But this time, Gabi turned to face him. "Do you have a better idea?" she asked boldly.

Someone else called out from the back of the room. "What are we going to paint?"

Principal Keystone looked thoughtful. Or was he frowning? Or was he falling asleep?

Everyone turned to stare at Gabi.

"Go ahead, Miss Rivera?" Principal Keystone prompted.

Genna nodded encouragingly to keep Gabi going.

"Um, what about, sort of, freshening up the school lobby? We could ... paint a mural on that big gray wall. And maybe some inspirational quotes in the stairwell? To encourage positive attitudes?"

"The inspirational quotes idea is awesome ..." someone said tentatively.

"And the mural!" Genna chimed in supportively.

"Like, a makeover?" Selfie Girl said snidely. There were snickers.

Gabi turned beet red. She hadn't realized that Selfie Girl was even in the room, but she knew that voice.

But Gabi took a deep breath and stood up. She grabbed a dry-erase marker and began to outline what she had in mind. First, she drew the outline of the school's front lobby. Bit by bit, she sketched possible ideas for the mural—arts, sports, academics, and other symbols of all the activities that make a school great.

"That's so cool," another kid said. "It really would be like a makeover. It would make the school look better."

It didn't take long before everyone in the room latched onto the idea of painting a mural in the lobby. Gabi was shocked. She'd dreamed about doing this for a very long time. But it was still really just an idea. Now she needed an actual plan.

She kept right on drawing on the white board. She finished up with the words *We Love PS 33!* in big letters. That was short for Public School 33.

"Whoa, you're a really good artist," some kid said.

Others murmured agreement, and Gabi bit her lip nervously, uncomfortable with compliments.

"Very impressive," Principal Keystone said, tapping his pen against his temple.

Kids started saying things like, "Yeah, that looks like fun!" and, "It will last longer than just one day," and, "Can I help too even though I'm bad at art?"

"That's the most important part," Gabi said bravely. "Everyone paints together. It's got to be a group effort."

"I think perhaps we've seized upon the best idea in the bunch," the principal said. "And your sketch really brings it to life. Thank you, Miss Rivera."

Gabi put down the marker. Kids were telling her

what they wanted to see on the mural. They wanted to know too, how long had she been drawing like this?

"You're the best artist in school," someone said.

Gabi turned and saw that it was Max. When did he walk in?

"Thanks," she said, feeling shy but also a teensy bit proud. She looked away from him. Those green eyes were staring right through her.

Awkward.

"Well, I think it's unanimous. The mural is a great way to improve school pride and positivity!" Principal Keystone sad. "And I love all the creativity the kids in this room have shown today."

Everyone chattered excitedly.

As the meeting concluded and the lunch bell rang, Gabi found herself in an unusual position: everyone was talking about her—but in a *good* way. She'd followed Daisy's advice about being true to herself—even though she wasn't entirely sure what that meant.

On the way home, Genna gave Gabi a double high-five. "This is going to be great. Let's stop in at Daisy's bakery to celebrate. Before we go up to your apartment, that is. Is your mom cool if we do that?"

"I think so!" Gabi said, with a *can-you-believe-it?* look on her face. So they swung inside the bakery doors. Gabi found a table while Genna went to use the restroom.

Unfortunately, Daisy wasn't in the shop. She'd gone out to a meeting of her own. Dina said there was a small business owner summit, and Daisy was a guest speaker.

"I bet she's an awesome speaker," Gabi said.

"Oh, she is!" Dina said. "She can really inspire a crowd!"

Dina walked away to get the French macarons that Genna had ordered. And then, like a lightning bolt from the blue, another brilliant idea zapped into Gabi's mind—one *more* thing they could do for positive attitudes.

"Genna," Gabi whispered excitedly when she returned. "I have the best idea."

"Another one? Your brain is overflowing."

"You know how Keystone said that thing about having motivational speakers come too? What if, along with doing the mural painting, we invited someone to come and talk to us about pride and positive thinking and stuff. Someone inspiring."

"Like who? Someone famous? Do famous people do that sort of thing? Wait, do you know someone famous that I don't know?"

Gabi chuckled. "This person isn't famous. Not exactly. But it's someone we both know."

Genna was stumped. "Give me a hint."

"She's someone who could cook up a fun talk for the students." Gabi giggled at her bad pun. "Get it? *Cook* up? This guest would be ... the frosting on our cake! Get it? Come on, bad-joke-queen! Guess!"

"Huh? What? I give up." Genna looked at Gabi like she was crazy.

"I'm talking about DAISY!"

Genna broke into a grin. "Oh! I get it. But does she do stuff like that?"

"I have no idea," Gabi confessed. "But Dina just said she was off giving a talk somewhere, so maybe. We have to ask her. She'd be the best, I just know it. Part of school pride is inspiration and confidence. Daisy gave a dose of that to me, right here, just this week."

In order to talk to Daisy, the girls waited around for her. Gabi called her mom to say that they were at the bakery. While they waited, the sky outside turned steely gray. A few moments later, something magical happened.

Snow.

"Look, Gabi!" Genna pointed out the large picture window at the shop.

It had begun to flake, just a little bit, like powdered sugar on the sidewalk.

Daisy finally returned in about half an half hour. The shop was bopping with people stopping into the bakery on their way home from the office, or families who had ventured outside to enjoy the snowfall. The streetlights gave the snow a magical sparkle.

"Talk about fairy dust!" Daisy laughed as she approached their table. She took off her mittens and scarf and playfully shook snowflakes on the girls. "Dina tells me you've been waiting to talk to me all this time?"

"Gabi is incredible!" Genna gushed. "She came up with this awesome idea for improving school spirit. But we need your help."

"Oh? My help? Do you need to make something in my kitchen?"

"Um," Gabi said quietly. "Not exactly. It's more like we need *you*."

"Me?"

"Do you think maybe you might be able to come to our school?"

"And do what?" Daisy looked perplexed.

"You could talk about Daisy's Desserts. About being true to yourself and believing in yourself?

About all the things you told me to make me feel better?"

"Well!" Daisy looked taken aback. "That's certainly an interesting idea."

"If the kids heard you, I know they'd catch school spirit," Gabi said. She explained how she wanted to inspire the whole school to work together to paint a lobby mural.

"Hmmm," Daisy murmured. "Now this project is intriguing me. I might have some idea about what I could say ..."

"There's only one catch. I just have to convince the principal that you're the perfect speaker for our spirit project," Gabi said.

"Maybe I need to bake him a big batch of apple bars to help persuade him?" Daisy joked.

Gabi threw her arms around Daisy. "Thank you!"

In that moment, in the middle of Daisy's Desserts, with the gentle snow falling outside, illuminated by the glow of the bakery's little lights, two friends and a magical baker launched a perfect pride and positivity campaign. Not only would PS 33 get a makeover. They'd get a great big *Bakeover*.

It was time to get to work.

Chapter 5

Half-Baked

Bzzzzzzzzzzzzzzzzzzz.

The doorbell rang, and Genna bounded into Gabi's apartment bearing gifts. "My mom made us some cut-up veggies and dip," Genna said, handing Gabi a plastic-wrapped tray.

"Better than my mom's gluten-free cookies," Gabi whispered.

"No doubt!" Genna snickered.

The girls logged onto Daisy's blog to see what they might find. The home page popped up with big pictures and a scrolling bar that showed a list of all the items in the bakery. They clicked through the entries, each one sounding yummier than the last.

"Chocolate babka!" Genna said. "My bubbe makes that. It's incredible!"

"Look at this! It's Daisy's biography." Gabi clicked the button.

<u>Name:</u> Daisy Jane Duncan

<u>Hometown:</u> All over with more destinations to come! Someday I would love to open a bakery in Greece or maybe China. My friend once showed me how to prepare the best Cantonese dim sum. I also love making steamed egg buns with sweet custard. May need to make a version for Daisy's Desserts ...

"What's a steamed egg bun?" Genna asked. "Wow, she really bakes everything, doesn't she?"

Gabi couldn't get enough of Daisy's blog posts, especially the internationally-themed ones. She scrolled through the site, pouring over each entry.

One post was about how to make the perfect donut.

Then there was one about what to do with all

those donut holes. The girls clicked with interest, thinking about getting some of those extra donut holes, and then busted out with embarrassed laughter when they realized it was a joke post. There *are* no leftover holes!

There were a few pages devoted to the hundreds of customizable cookie types that Daisy's offered, which included options for size and shape as well as flavor.

"If I had to make the perfect cookie, I'd make a triangular oatmeal cookie with currants," Gabi said. "Nut-free, chewy, delicious!"

"I would make a double fudge cookie with chocolate mini-chips dipped in chocolate with chocolate sprinkles on top." Genna laughed. "And I don't care what shape they come in as long as they're chocolate!"

"Hey, check this out," Gabi clicked a blog post that started with a clipping from an old newspaper article with a cluster of cake riddles.

CAKE RIDDLES
What kind of cake would you use for a bath? Sponge cake.
What kind of cake do bats like? Upside down cake.
What type of cake weighs itself? Pound cake …

You Take the Cake!

Last weekend, Dina and I stayed late on a Thursday because the ovens were acting up. We have about ten different kinds of bread we bake very early every morning, but if the ovens are not working properly, it throws off our entire schedule. It's a little bit like "Night at the Museum" inside Daisy's Desserts on nights like this—some of the items on display seem to come to life! We're so tired we sometimes think we hear whispers and make up stories about the after-hours "visitors," each with a sweet tooth for all of our treats …

They scrolled through a bunch of other postings before finally landing on a page of photographs. There was a picture of Daisy as a baby in her high chair with cake smashed all over her face and hands. She was grinning from ear to ear. Her head was a shock of adorable carrot orange. From the start, she'd been a genuine redhead.

The slide show began to play as Gabi and Genna

kept clicking through. There was some kind of jazz music playing in the background. There were funny photos of Daisy at about the girls' age, sitting in front of a birthday cake that looked like it was lopsided. Then there were a couple of pictures of Daisy in chef-whites, working as a line cook in some expensive restaurant, standing in front of a gigantic fork and spoon sculpture, and hanging out in a backyard with a gigantic, melting ice cream sandwich in her hand.

"She always seems so happy," Genna pointed out.

"Yeah. I think she really knows a lot about positive attitudes. I think everyone at our school could take a lesson from her."

Gabi's mom appeared in Gabi's doorway after a while. "Are you girls planning on heading over to the bakery again?"

"Well, we do need to do more *research*," Genna teased, using air quotes. "Though I've got to run. My cousins are in town."

"But I'm going, Mamá," Gabi said. "Okay?"

"You might as well move in there," Gabi's mom said, shaking her head. "But hey, while you're there, why don't you pick us up some of those peanut-free treats you said she was trying out."

"Really, Mamá?" Gabi asked, surprised. She and Genna exchanged a shocked look.

Gabi's mom nodded. "Sure. Let's give them a try."

Gabi decided not to question this change of heart her mom seemed to have about letting Gabi have more freedom. She was just riding it like a wave. Or, like an ice rink. There was, after all, massive snow in the forecast. The recent light dusting was only the big tease. Gabi knew all about being teased. But she was beginning to think that maybe she was more prepared for the big storm than she thought.

The girls threw on their sweatshirts and jackets and headed out. "I promise I'll be home in about an hour," Gabi said as she stepped onto the elevator.

Genna headed for home and Gabi dashed

across the street to Daisy's. She never expected to get the royal treatment, but that's how it went. She walked inside, the door jangled, and then Babs and Dina swooped over and took Gabi by the arm. "Our allergy-free kitchen is ready!" Dina sang. They told Gabi to head into the back of the bakery for a special treat. That was for starters.

Gabi was thrilled to see a table of treats just waiting to be sampled. And her special treat was definitely nut free *and* gluten free—it was an awesome puffed rice treat with one end dunked in rich, dark, chocolate. She took a big, delicious bite. "This is the best thing ever," Gabi announced as she crunched. "Safe to eat and perfectly sweet!"

"Aha! Our first taste tester!" Daisy said, strolling over. "Check out our special areas of the kitchen, reserved for allergy-free food prep. We had a consultant come in today, and we passed inspection! Eggs, nuts, dairy, gluten—we've got it covered! And you really helped me out with this, Gabi."

Gabi was speechless. To think that someone

had gone out of the way to help people like her was overwhelming to think about.

Daisy brought out some notes. She had been brainstorming about what her presentation for the "bakeover" would include. She said she could talk about how she worked really hard to achieve her goal, even though there were lots of obstacles along the way. (A shortage of money to get started, a shoulder surgery that kept her out of the kitchen for nearly a year, and the death of her beloved Nana Belle that threw her into a tailspin, to name a few.)

She also planned to talk about team spirit, telling how she formed her baking team and how they always had one another's backs. And, most importantly, how, if she hadn't believed she could do it, she never would have opened her own bakery.

Then for some fun stuff! Gabi peeked at the list of ideas Daisy had come up with for possible activities to include in her presentation.

"Maybe I'll start off with some funny questions, or tell a few cake riddles ..."

"Hey! We saw those on your blog!" Gabi said.

Daisy grinned. "You're good. You've been doing some research, huh? Oh, that reminds me. Gabi, do you think maybe you could help me with a little something too?"

Gabi brightened right up. "I could try. What do you need?"

"Artwork."

"What do you mean?"

"Dina showed me the art you drew on the table-cloth," Daisy said.

"Oh," Gabi said. "Was it okay that I did that? I mean you *did* leave out cups of crayons ..."

"More than okay! It was brilliant. But it got me thinking that maybe after the big bakeover event, you can help me with some artwork here at the bakeshop? Of course I'd pay you, and that would officially make you a *professional* artist."

Gabi's eyes went wide. "You want *me* to draw for you?"

Daisy had just asked her to do the thing she

loved more than anything else on Earth. She wanted to scream, "YES, YES, YES!"

"I want to redo the menus featuring art of all our favorite items." Daisy stood up. "I think you're more than capable. From what I saw, you can draw anything. You have a special way of looking at the world."

"I do?" Gabi blushed.

"That's what I see," Daisy said. "You have to decide what you see for yourself."

Chapter 6

Frosties

Later that week Gabi could hardly sleep. She heard the wind outside, whipping around at the edges of her windowpanes. Happily, she was going over recent events in her mind: visiting Daisy; the offer to do art for her menus; and a new sort of mom who wasn't as fiercely overprotective this week as she seemed last week. Gabi could really get used to the new version.

In the middle of the night, Gabi was still awake. Her mind was racing. So much had been happening. Had it all begun with Genna's love of dessert? Yep, dessert and a boring assembly in the school auditorium. Sometimes it was funny how life worked.

Then there was the new boy, Max. Gabi thought about him too much and was afraid to wonder what he thought of her after the hot cocoa fiasco at the bakery.

And of course there was this crazy bakery lady, Daisy, who seemed to be opening Gabi's mind in all sorts of ways.

And finally there was the spirit project at school. Her idea had been chosen out of the whole bunch. *Hers!* When she had met with Principal Keystone to ask him about having Daisy come speak, he agreed. It didn't even take as much convincing as she thought it would. Score!

"And I love that mural idea," Principal Keystone had said to Gabi. "You're really on to something there. That's leadership thinking, Miss Rivera. And maybe when this is all done, we'll look into starting an art club."

Gabi took it all in. It felt like her world was

suddenly getting so much bigger than it had been just last week. Bigger ... and better.

She'd worked with Principal Keystone to discuss ideas for the assembly with Daisy. Then they had talked more about her mural idea and how every-one—every student in the school!—would help complete it by painting different sections. It would be a true team effort.

Now she lay there in the dark, checking her phone so much she was literally watching time pass. She was too excited to sleep. Then her stomach began talking to her, growling loudly, so Gabi got up and out of bed and headed for the refrigerator. She'd brought home a box of safe-to-eat treats from Daisy's Desserts. That would make an inappropri-ate, but perfect, middle-of-the-night snack. Now, where was that box?

"Gab?" A voice came from the dark on the other side of the kitchen.

"Ah!" Gabi yelped and jumped about a mile.

Leo appeared around the refrigerator door.

"Sheesh, Leo! You scared me to death!"

"Sorry, hon. What are you doing up at this hour?"

"I might ask you the same thing," Gabi said, pointing to the box in Leo's hand. It was the treats from Daisy's!

"Did you bring these home?" Leo asked. "Because they were delicious."

"*Were*? Leo, you ate them all?"

Leo chuckled. "I had *one* mini-éclair. And don't tell your mom, because even though they're nut -free, I'm pretty sure they're not calorie-free. You want one?"

They sat together in the moonlit kitchen, sampling the guaranteed nut-free goodies, and drinking warm milk together.

"So, it's been a crazy week, huh?" Leo asked. He stuck his finger inside another éclair to get a scoop of custard.

"That's an understatement," Gabi said with a yawn.

"How are your grades?" Leo asked.

"Mamá says they're just 'okay,'" Gabi said. "But that's because an A isn't as good as an A+. She's pretty tough on me, in case you haven't noticed."

"She means well," Leo said. "You know she just worries about you and wants what's best for you."

"I know," Gabi sighed. "She's been different lately, though. Like, actually trusting me to make my own decisions, you know?"

Leo smiled and tugged on Gabi's long brown hair. "She also told me that you've really begun to speak out about your ideas, especially with this big project."

"She told you that?"

Leo nodded. "You know how proud we are of you, right Gab?"

Gabi shrugged.

"It wasn't very long ago that you would hardly speak in front of anyone. You're really growing up ... becoming who you are meant to be."

"Okay, okay, no need to get mushy about it!" Gabi protested.

"Anyone teasing you lately?" Leo asked gently.

"One girl last week kind of hassled me, and then she sort of rolled her eyes about my idea in the school-spirit meeting. But you know what? No one really listened to her. When other kids said that my idea was good, the mean girl just shut up. That was kind of nice."

"Sooner or later, people start to realize that people like that aren't so funny. And when the audience stops laughing, the mean kids usually give up," Leo said. He rapped one knuckle on Gabi's head and stood up. "Back to bed with you."

They both yawned and shuffled back to their bedrooms. A few hours later, when her alarm clock belted out its alien beeping, Gabi leaped out of bed, got dressed, and faced the new day. She was exhausted, but also energized somehow. She had a lot of work to do, and she felt ready.

She pictured Daisy running around her bakery, actively involved in everything around her. That's how Gabi was starting to feel, and it was great.

Like people were hearing her and seeing her in a whole new way.

Out the window, Gabi spotted a couple of enormous hanging icicles. When she drew back the curtain, she found something even more surprising: Snow—and lots of it. The city was dusted white all over. On the street she saw people bundled up in black coats and hustling from corner to corner.

It looked like several inches had fallen, and people were looking around in wonder as they walked down the street. Gabi was excited to pull on her giant snow boots, which had been locked in the closet all winter, just waiting for a day like this.

She dressed in a warm woolen sweater and jeans, pushed her newly dip-dyed purple hair into a pair of chopsticks, and poured herself an overflowing bowl of Frosties, the best cereal in the whole wide world because the company made everything on nut-free equipment.

While packing her book bag for school, Gabi realized to her dismay that she hadn't finished up a math problem set. *I could have been doing that at four in the morning instead of eating éclairs!* she thought.

She tried to do it at the kitchen table. Of course whenever Mom caught her doing last-minute work, she got on Gabi's case about procrastinating.

But today Mom couldn't stay mad for long. In fact, she had a reason to be *proud* of Gabi right now. Earlier that morning, Principal Keystone had called to confirm that the school would be hosting an event that Gabi had suggested: inviting a guest speaker to improve school morale—and getting the students to paint an inspirational mural in the lobby. The principal had just wanted to make sure that Gabi's parents would give their permission for Gabi to have her photograph taken by any media sources covering the story.

Mom was delighted to say yes, of course. But no one bothered to ask Gabi, the allergic girl who was much happier staying in the background, if *she* would like being photographed. Gabi was used to being invisible. She wasn't at all sure she was ready to be in the spotlight.

But once she got to school, Gabi threw herself into her work. Genna was home with a cold, so she wasn't in homeroom. That meant a much quieter school day without a BFF to gossip with between classes.

The English teacher wanted the class to continue reading *The Outsiders*. Gabi had already read ahead to the end of the book. It made her cry, but she couldn't spoil it for everyone else, so she kept mum. She had loads on her mind anyway. Could she fake her way through today's class period?

But then the teacher asked an interesting question: "Are you a Greaser or a Soc?"

The kids had to choose one group from the novel.

Gabi chose a Greaser. Because she was the outsider, not the cool girl.

Selfie Girl chose Soc. Because of course.

The teacher asked the students if they liked to

be put into a specific category, or if they liked it better when there was no label on them.

Did Gabi have a label? If she did, it was probably dork. But then she thought about Daisy saying that she was "queen of the dorks," and Gabi smiled. She was happy to be in the same "club" as Daisy.

And Gabi decided that if being good at art and dressing in her own unique way and even having allergies were what made people think she was a dork, then so be it. She was those things and so many more, and they made her who she was.

Next the teacher challenged her students to write an "I AM POEM." The goal of the poem was to see what students find most interesting about themselves.

Gabi groaned a little bit when she heard the word P-O-E-M. She liked stories, and she loved drawing, of course. But she didn't really get poems. She sometimes felt that when she started into a poem she got lost, tripped over a few words, and ended up in a dark forest without any bread crumbs.

Nonetheless, she looked over the sheet and began to fill in the blanks.

Or tried to, anyway.

"I Am" Poem

I am _____ creative & quirky??? _____
(Two special characteristics)

I wonder____ why I see the world this way I do ____
(Something you are curious about)

I hear _____ snow whistling _____
(An imaginary sound)

I see_____ a frozen marshmallow sky _____
(An imaginary sight)

I want_____ to leap into a cloud _____
(A desire you have)

I pretend____ to be interested _____
(Pretend to do this)

I worry _about ~~not being enough~~ all the snow melting_
(something that bothers you)

I cry____ being the outsider _____
(Something that makes you sad)

I am____ creative & curious!!! _____
(The first line of the poem repeated)

I understand __ that happiness is a nut-free
frosted cupcake __
(Something you know is true)

I say____ we all have something to offer _____
(Something you believe in)

I dream_____ *of colorful fabrics*_____
(Something you dream about)

I try_____ *to make my mom happy*_____
(Something you make an effort on)

I hope_____ *I get guts*_____
(Something you hope for)

I am_____ *creative & ~~curious~~ very, very brave*_____
(The first line of the poem repeated)

After language arts, Gabi was surprised to hear her named being called on the intercom. She was to report to Principal Keystone's office. Gabi had never been called to the principal's office before, but she wasn't too worried. Maybe that media guy was there to take her picture already?

She hurried down to Principal Keystone's office. The assistant told Gabi to go right in, and she found the principal watering his plants.

"Ah, Gabi! Thanks for stopping in. I don't want to keep you too long from your next class, but I just wanted to give you a head's up that we'll be teaming you up with another student on the mural project.

She's one of the best artists in the seventh grade and, in fact, won a contest this fall for a portrait she painted. She expressed interest in helping out with this mural project, and I thought it would be great for you two to work as partners."

Gabi listened, nodding. She had hoped that she might be able to ask if Genna could help out with the design, but even Gabi had to admit that Genna's art skills weren't great.

"Oh, here she is!" Principal Keystone said, looking toward the door. "Gabi, have you met Annie Sloane?"

Gabi looked to the door to meet her new partner and found herself face to face with Selfie Girl.

Chapter 7

D is for Donuts

"What!?" Genna said when Gabi told her what had happened. "You have to work with her? This is crazy!"

"I know!" Gabi moaned. "What do I do?"

"Kill her with kindness?" Genna suggested. "That's what my mom always says."

"What does that even mean, anyway?"

"You know, take the high road, pretend everything is great, and be really nice to her so that she can't possibly be mean back to you," Genna explained.

"But what if she doesn't deserve it?" Gabi asked.

"That's all I got," Genna said, shrugging.

Gabi sighed. Luckily, she had other things to occupy her mind: The Bakeover. Part One was Daisy's presentation, and that was coming up soon. She was busy helping Daisy with the plan and making sure everything she needed would be ready at the school. Part Two was the mural painting, which would happen a couple of weeks later. Gabi would have to meet with Selfie Girl ... Annie ... to finalize the design and get it approved by Principal Keystone. She wasn't looking forward to that.

Now, more than ever, Gabi hoped that the Bakeover would have the power to change everything—and everyone—for the better. Like how she had felt when she'd first stepped into Daisy's Desserts.

Genna and Gabi ended up making most of the posters announcing Daisy's visit to school. They also worked with the art teacher to make an enormous banner that hung on the stage where Daisy would be speaking.

WELCOME DAISY'S DESSERTS!

To say Principal Keystone was impressed was an understatement. He was *amazed* that Gabi, who barely spoke in classrooms, was now running a major event like this (with the help of lots of others, of course). But as usual, Gabi was content to work behind the scenes.

Before Gabi knew it, Part One of the Bakeover had arrived. Daisy came to the school and Gabi, Genna, and Principal Keystone were waiting in the school lobby to greet her. The girls helped Daisy carry in all her gear and goodies and helped get the stage set up for her. At ten o'clock, the loudspeaker announced that everyone was dismissed to assembly. It was time!

"Settle down, students!" Principal Keystone boomed when they were ready to begin.

Gabi and Genna sat in the front row so they could have a close-up view of Daisy. Her hair was exceptionally frizzy today, and Gabi loved it. Knowing that that was what Daisy had least liked about herself, and that it was now one of the things she loved most, made Gabi love it too. Daisy was wearing one of her custom aprons from the bakery, and she was up on stage behind a long table preparing the samples and mixing ingredients into small bowls. Gabi couldn't wait to see how the students reacted to Daisy's inspirational message.

"This is awesome," Genna whispered to Gabi when Daisy was introduced. "I can't believe we made this happen!"

"Well, technically *she* is making it happen," Gabi corrected her friend. "But I think we do deserve *some* of the credit. Thanks for making me speak up in the first place."

"You're welcome," Genna said. "Of course, I knew there'd be some dessert in it for me too," she teased.

Gabi looked around the room. Kids were jumping around in their seats, and the volume was pumped up high from one row to the next. Was *this* the spirit that the principal had wanted to get into the school?

"Good morning everybody!" Daisy sang out.

Everyone started to clap, Gabi and Genna loudest of all.

The presentation started a little slowly, but soon Daisy began inviting students up on stage. After asking if her volunteers had food allergies or any other food restrictions, she gave them each a chef's hat and asked if they were willing to put their taste buds to the test. Daisy made a point of saying that everything she brought along was one-hundred percent nut free. Gabi smiled gratefully—not that she was planning on volunteering to go on stage!

Daisy handed one girl a muffin that looked like chocolate chip. She took a bite and her eyebrows shot up in surprise. The chocolate chips were actually beef jerky bits! Daisy gave another student a pretzel and what looked like cheese dip, but which was actually orange frosting. Her point? "Keep your mind open and don't make assumptions based just on what you see. This applies to food, people, activities, everything!" Daisy said. "What if you want to try a new class or join a new club, but you don't know anyone in it? Just give it a try. You never know when or where you're going to make a new best friend or find a lifelong hobby."

Then Daisy brought out a whole tray of colorful treats. "And you also have to be persistent," she continued. "You may not find a friend you click with right away, or the field that's going to become your future career, until you try *a lot* of options. Like all of these options." She held out the tray of unusual cookies for all to see.

A boy named Josh was her next volunteer. He shoved his hands into his pockets, trying to act cool. "Josh, would you do me the honor of inviting up a pair of friends? We are going to play a little game."

Josh called out, "Max and Annie!" Gabi got butterflies as she watched Max walk to the front of the room ... followed by her new "partner," Annie.

Everyone was on the edge of their seat. "I want you three students to be very brave. Can you do that?" Daisy asked. All three nodded nervously.

Daisy instructed Annie to choose one cookie for herself, and two more cookies for Max and Josh.

Annie got a mischievous look in her eye and selected an ugly brown cookie for Max, a strange orange cookie for Josh, and a beautifully decorated and frosted pink cookie for herself. They were each to taste their cookie and identify the flavor.

Max went first. He took a tentative bite and said, "Cinnamon?" Daisy gave him the thumbs up and asked Josh to go next.

Josh took a big, brave bite and chewed thoughtfully. "Caramel?" he finally said.

"Bravo!" Daisy clapped. Annie was next.

She took a bite of the yummy-looking pink concoction and chewed for two seconds before putting her hand to her mouth and spitting it back out.

"Not what you expected?" Daisy asked.

Annie shook her head fiercely.

"Can you identify the flavor?"

"Garlic?" she asked, wrinkling her nose.

"Bingo! You guys are good at this game!" Daisy

winked at the audience. "Any lessons we can take from this, audience?"

"Don't volunteer to eat strange cookies?" a smart alec yelled. Everyone laughed.

Gabi was surprised to see Genna boldly raise her hand. "Don't judge a book by its cover—or a cookie by its appearance?"

"Aha!" Daisy said. "Yes! Good things come in all kinds of packages. And sometimes, the fanciest packages are surprisingly deceptive." She raised her eyebrows twice and thanked the three students. Josh and Max high-fived as they stepped off the stage, and Annie made an exaggerated gagging motion to make her friends laugh.

Gabi nudged Genna and giggled. This was going even better than they thought.

Even though everyone now understood the game, they were still eager to give it a try. Several more volunteers took their turns tasting the mystery cookies. The lucky ones got chocolate or strawberry. The unlucky ones got cayenne pepper, minty dental floss, and other disgusting flavors. The kid who got the cayenne pepper starting running around the stage like a chicken. Everyone roared with laughter. Daisy was a master at orchestrating it all.

After a while, Daisy slowed down the games. She told the basic story of how the bakery began and how her Nana Belle inspired her. This was mostly stuff that Gabi had read online, but still, she hung on every word Daisy said. It was amazing to hear all that Daisy had experienced to get where she was.

Daisy came down to the foot of the stage and sat down with the mic in her hand.

And that's when something shifted. That was when *everything* shifted.

Gabi had seen it happen inside the bakery. Now she was witnessing the same change right here at school. It wasn't magic, not exactly. There were no magic wands or spells. There was just a feeling—a feeling that hung over the room like a fairy-dust fog, like a trance.

Gabi turned to glance around the entire auditorium as Daisy spoke. Kids who normally would have been bouncing out of their seats were not doing that now. They weren't whispering or shouting out. No one was yelling or teasing. The row of Annie's friends even stopped chattering. Gabi saw Max out of the corner of her eye. He was looking at Daisy too.

The lights dimmed just a little bit while Daisy went on with her speech using a PowerPoint display behind her with funny pictures of kitchen disasters and baking fails.

"A few thoughts about things I've learned being a baker: Number one. Remember to have patience. If you keep checking the muffin tin every five minutes while it's baking, the muffins won't cook any faster. What does this mean for you? Don't rush things, students. Everything in its own time.

"Number two. Try new things! Don't knock it 'til you've tried it. I used to think that I'd never master the perfect merengue. And you know? I didn't—not for quite a while! But with a lot of work, I finally did it. Now I'll challenge anyone to out-merengue me! Another example: I used to think that I hated bananas. But I had a friend who was sick, and the only thing she said she could eat was banana bread. Well, I held my nose and mushed up those bananas and made my first-ever loaf of banana bread. And you know what? *I loved it!* I ate all of it myself and had to make another loaf for my friend!" Daisy laughed as a picture went up on the screen showing her holding a banana in front of her face in the shape of a smile.

"Number three. Impossible is what no one else has done, until someone finally does it. For me, this is how I feel about mixing flavors or testing out new recipes. There are no set rules. Make it up as you go along. Be brave enough to tackle big, difficult things. Do you think we put a human on the moon by saying, 'Gee, that sounds too hard'?"

"And finally, number four. Take pride. Take pride in yourself, in your school, in your family, in your group. If you're not doing something with your life that makes you proud, make a change. Take a stand. Be brave enough to say, "Yeah, I *love* chemistry, and I'm proud of that. Or I *love* art, and I'm really good at it!" With this, Daisy looked right at Gabi and gave a small smile. "And you should love this school! Because in a few short years, you'll be moving on. This is the only time in your life that you'll be this age. Enjoy it. Embrace it. And make it a worthy experience—not just one to be suffered through. This is your chance to make a positive difference."

Everyone gave a loud cheer.

"Sometimes, in the middle of a day when everything seems to be going against you, remember the three Ds. Do you know what the Ds are? Any ideas?"

"Daisy's Desserts?" someone called out.

"Congrats—you know your letters ... but not your numbers. That was only two! And no, that's not what I meant," Daisy teased.

No one raised their hand at first, but then, one by one, kids began to offer suggestions.

"Dreams?" one kid shouted out.

"Yes! Dreams! You need to always remember to dream big. I came here to speak to you about baking, but not in the way you think. Baking is *my* dream. You have to find your own dream. What other Ds do you know?"

"Dopey?"

"Dorks!!"

A few kids laughed at the silly answers, but not as many as in a typical assembly. People seemed to actually want to hear what Daisy had to say. Then a kid in the back of the auditorium called out, "Determination?"

"YES! Who said that?" Daisy cried. She pointed to the back. "That's a smart kid back there!"

"D is also for Donuts! Do you have any of those?" someone else called out.

"Next time I'll bring donuts." Daisy laughed.

Gabi saw Principal Keystone smiling. Daisy had the room in her hands, and she wasn't letting go. Eventually she got the kids to identify that third D too: Desire.

"So why is school pride and spirit important?" Daisy asked the room.

The room was silent. No snarky answers this time.

"It's important because spirit empowers us. It opens doors for us. It brings us closer to one another. It creates a community. This is *your* community, so make it a good one! Thanks for listening, everyone!" Daisy ended, and everyone cheered.

"Students!" Principal Keystone was back at the mic. "We have one more activity with Ms. Duncan. She will be doing a cooking demo in the cafeteria. Please gather in groups with your homerooms. And now, let's show Ms. Duncan that school spirit, shall we?"

Everyone cheered and clapped again. As the auditorium began to clear out, some kids came up to thank Gabi for inviting Daisy to speak. She was overwhelmed by the whole scene. She couldn't believe that she had helped make this happen, and that she wasn't invisible for once. It felt pretty good.

Gabi lurked in the background before the demonstration began, waiting for her turn to talk to Daisy. She couldn't get a word in edgewise. People were swarming around Daisy.

Gabi noticed that several of the other girls in her class seemed to already know Daisy too. They rushed over to her for hugs. Gabi felt a little stab of jealousy when she saw them acting so friendly. She secretly wished that she could have Daisy all to herself—or at least to share with Genna only. Instead, she watched as a nice girl named Emme and the math-genius-girl Kiki monopolized the amazing Daisy Duncan.

Gabi finally got up her nerve to plow through the crowd. "Excuse me," she said politely, but forcefully. "I need to talk to Daisy now. Sorry!"

Daisy gave Gabi an impressed look. "That was marvelous," she complimented her. "You spoke up for yourself. You made yourself *heard*! Way to go!"

"Did you meet those girls at your bakery?" Gabi asked, nodding toward Emme and Kiki, who had backed away to let Gabi talk with Daisy. Gabi was sort of the master of ceremonies, after all!

"I sure did. Everyone has a different and important reason for showing up at my bakery—and I welcome every one of them."

"When I first met you," Gabi said, "I felt like you could almost read my mind. Can you?"

Daisy chuckled. "Well, everyone can if they pay close enough attention. It's just called listening!"

Across the corridor, a news reporter had been waiting for a quote and possibly a photo of Daisy and Gabi. Since Daisy was busy getting ready for her demonstration, she didn't have much time to talk. "Why don't you go talk to them?" she asked Gabi.

"What?" Gabi started to hyperventilate a little at the thought of talking to a news reporter, but then she remembered one of Daisy's very own Ds. Determination! And she thought about her *abuela*, "walking tall." Gabi had to speak up and out. She took a deep breath and approached the reporter.

"Hi! I'm Gabi," she said, boldly. Proudly.

"Just the person I wanted to talk to!" the reporter said. He asked some basic questions, and Gabi answered. It wasn't hard at all!

About her favorite items in the bake shop ... *chocolate éclairs, of course. And all the other nut-free options!*

About what made the bakery such a great place ... *the people! Especially everyone on Daisy's team.*

About how Daisy was helping with positive attitudes and school spirit ... *because Daisy had more spirit and a brighter attitude than just about anyone else in the world!*

The more she spoke, the more comfortable she got. Gabi finished up by telling the reporter about the second phase of their spirit rally in a few weeks—the mural!

That was the part where Gabi would really have to shine. She just hoped she could still "shine" in the shadow of Miss Selfie.

Chapter 8

A Sour Surprise

"… We invited our local baker to present to the student body," said Principal Keystone from Public School 33. "She blew us away. Not only did she give our students a much needed dose of pride and spirit, but she showed the students what can happen if they follow their dreams." The Principal then added, "Of course, the most important thing is to stay in school and get an education."

"Daisy is a huge inspiration," said Gabriela Rivera, sixth-grade student at PS 33. "She is more than just a baker. She takes care of people's hearts as well as their tummies. She makes me believe I can do anything …"

Wow! Gabi couldn't believe the newspaper article when it was printed the following day. She read the article three times. Her name was right there in black and white—and right next to Daisy's! Did this make Gabi a little bit famous? It hadn't been as awkward as she thought it would, being in front of

121

strangers and having to speak out about how she felt or what her opinion was. Some of her super-shyness had to drop away ... and it had. This was a major accomplishment.

Gabi's mom and Leo were so proud of her, they could hardly contain themselves. They called everyone they knew to share the news and promised to send them all pictures of the mural when it was complete. Gabi was a little embarrassed, but also proud, herself. Her invisibility shield seemed to be falling away too.

Another snowstorm blew into town, and the temperatures dipped again. Carlos put up heavy velvet curtains at the front of the bakery to keep out the drafts. They put down runners on the floor to try to keep the place cozy. Orders for all kinds of tea and hot cocoa went through the roof. Everyone was doing whatever they could to stay warm. Business usually slowed down a little bit when the weather got icy. But Daisy's Desserts seemed to have *more* customers than ever.

Gabi came in several times to work on the art for the new menu. Genna came along too, to do her homework in the back (and grab something sweet right out of the oven—she was sneaky like that!).

Sometimes Gabi's mom would even stop in. She and Daisy were friends now too. Daisy had been showing Gabi's mom all kinds of secrets to make gluten-free baking taste even better.

Daisy was a very mellowing influence on things somehow. Gabi didn't feel like her mother was forever hovering over her at every moment. She wasn't putting strict limitations on Gabi anymore. She was learning to trust people and to trust Gabi's own instincts. In fact, her mom was *encouraging* Gabi to do things on her own, to take risks, to follow her dreams. Gabi felt like not only was the rest of the world starting to listen to what she had to say, but most important of all, her mom was listening too.

Of course, Gabi knew Leo also had something to do with all this. He never doubted her ability to take charge. Gabi always wondered how life delivered the things she needed at the exact moments when she needed them: Leo as a Dad and her biggest fan; Genna as the best BFF anyone ever had; and Daisy, arriving in Gabi's life with allergy-free sprinkles and powdered sugar, who saw something in Gabi that she hadn't been able to see for herself.

But Gabi still had another hurdle to face: Annie. She'd put it off for long enough, and she couldn't delay the meeting any longer. Gabi finally got up the nerve to approach Annie in language arts and ask if she'd meet her that afternoon at Daisy's. Annie had pulled her attention away from her friends long enough to say, "Yeah, sure. See you there."

Ugh.

Right after school, Gabi zipped over to Daisy's to get a table and mentally prepare herself. She thought about the advice everyone had given her. Genna, Mom, Leo, and Daisy had all weighed in with suggestions for dealing with Annie and utilizing some of that "positive attitude" this whole project was about.

Several minutes late, Annie blew in with the snow. Gabi was surprised to see that she had stacks of papers and folders that seemed to all be covered with sketches. "Hi, Gabi!" she said cheerily, as if they were best friends, and plopped down in the chair across from her. "So, I've got a bunch of ideas for us, and I think it's going to be really awesome ..."

Barely coming up for air, Annie dove right in about her big idea for the mural: She wanted to paint the Greasers and Socs from *The Outsiders.*

Annie wanted to paint a mural in the school of ... two rival gangs?

Gabi was dumbfounded. How did *that* convey school spirit and positive attitudes?

"So, I think I've got it all figured out. I'll just run this by Principal Keystone tomorrow, and we'll be good to go. Okay?" Annie finished her speech and began piling up her sketches as quickly as she had spread them out.

Gabi knew she had to do something, had to say something, now. This was not her vision.

She couldn't let Annie take over like this. "I don't think ..." Gabi began, licking her lips as she collected her thoughts.

Out of the corner of her eye, she caught a glimpse of Max. He was sitting a few tables away, doing his homework but peeking sideways at them. Then she saw Daisy up at the counter, who was nodding encouragingly at her. She felt a surge of confidence.

"No, Annie, I don't think that will work with the theme of the project. I think we need to show togetherness ... instead of separateness, you know?"

Annie looked at her quizzically but said nothing.

Gabi took a deep breath. "Let me show you my idea," she said and pulled out her own stacks of sketches. She spread them out in front of Annie and waited for her response.

Annie looked at them carefully for a moment without saying a word. Then she looked up at Gabi, and a slow smile spread across her face. "I hate to admit it, but I kind of love it," she said.

Gabi nearly fell out of her chair in shock.

Was it possible that Annie was a reasonable human being?

But then Annie added, "It's pretty complicated, though. Can we pull it off?"

That was a good question. This was going to take *a lot* of positive thinking.

Chapter 9

Everything Snowballs

Every minute that Gabi was not working on the mural design or on her homework, she was working on her sketches for Daisy's menus. She had never been so busy in her life, and she was loving every minute of it.

Some of what Gabi decided to draw for the menus made everyone laugh, because it was so unexpected: bakers on roller skates; a pair of fluffy pups waiting outside and getting a surprise treat from Carlos; Babs modeling at least five different movie-star quality outfits, all complete with her signature apron. There were smaller sketches of pastries and cakes too, with cookie cutouts of every shape imaginable, including stars, diamonds, and hearts.

One afternoon at the shop, Gabi and Genna sneaked into the kitchen, and Carlos showed them how to make an allergy-friendly sweet treat called snowballs, fitting for the weather. He started with a batch of puffed rice and mixed in butter and melted marshmallows—*homemade* marshmallows to boot! Once it was mixed together, he shaped the mixture into small, snowball-sized orbs. Then, when they were cooled, he dipped half of each ball into melted white chocolate. It was *snow* fabulous. He rolled some of the balls in rock sugar too. Or mixed mini-chocolate-chips in with the puffed rice mixture. No matter what the variation, the very best part about these snowballs was the obvious: They were Gabi-friendly!

Perfection!

On the afternoon before Bakeover Part Two (the big mural painting!), Gabi and Genna took over a table in the corner of the bakery. There was pop music playing in the background, and they were working on their science lab together. Gabi was telling Genna for the hundredth time that no, she wouldn't reveal the secret mural design! She was sworn to secrecy. Genna was persistent, as always, but Gabi wouldn't give in this time. But she did promise Genna that she would love the end result.

Gabi and Annie had been going in early to school most mornings to work on putting the sketch framework up on the wall for all the other students to paint. Before the morning bell rang, the girls would tape large pieces of paper over the sketch to hide it from the other students, hoping to keep it a surprise for the big day.

Genna was baffled that Gabi didn't seem to *hate* working with Annie.

"Annie and I have come to an understanding," was the only way that Gabi could explain it. Gabi and Annie somehow worked okay together. Actually, they fought together too, but in a good way. There were certainly times when Gabi wanted things one way, and Annie wanted them another way, and one or the other would have to give in. But Gabi felt really good about the fact that she only had to give in *some* of the time, not *all* the time. She was walking tall, and it felt great!

Of course, Gabi didn't think she and Annie would ever be real friends, and that was okay too. But they were partners. Gabi wasn't invisible, and she was making her voice be heard.

"You go girl!" Genna was saying to Gabi when the bell on the shop door jangled.

And in walked Max.

"Alert," Genna said, sitting up straight. "Max is in the house."

He was with a big group of kids, as usual. They sat on the other side of the bakery. At first, it didn't seem like he even noticed Gabi and Genna.

"Aren't you going to say hello?" Genna asked, poking Gabi.

"If he comes over I guess," Gabi said. "Whatever. Boys are dumb."

"I thought you sort of liked him? He seemed nice."

Gabi frowned. "Max probably has every girl in our class crushing on him. Why would I matter?" Even though Gabi was feeling more confident about a lot of things these days , she wasn't feeling that way about Max.

Babs swung by the table and admired some doodles that Gabi had drawn on the tablecloth again. Unconscious habit. Now, no matter where she went, Gabi couldn't help but draw. She was lucky though, to have her art. It was helping her more and more to figure out how she was feeling. It was helping her say what she needed to say.

"You have a real eye for detail, m'dear," Babs said sweetly. "Having you girls around this place has been real special for us. You know that?"

Gabi smiled. "Thanks, Babs."

Babs cleared away one of the plates and headed toward Max's table. Gabi caught a glimpse of him.

But when she looked at him, he looked at her. At the exact same time. *Great.*

But he surprised Gabi by waving. Then he got up. *Double great.*

"I guess he knows you're here," Genna teased. She turned toward Max as he walked over.

"Hey, Gabriela," Max said. "Haven't seen you around much lately."

"Yeah, I guess I've been busy. You good?"

"Yeah. Sure. Hey, big day tomorrow, right? Save me a good spot to paint on the mural, will you?" He smiled.

"Yeah," Gabi said. "Sure."

Genna made a face. "Do you want to sit with us?" she asked.

"No, uh ..." Max stammered. "I have to get back to my friends."

"Your friends?" Genna repeated. "Right. Better hurry back to them."

"See you tomorrow," Gabi said.

Max tapped the table and then turned to head back to his seat. He looked one more time, over his shoulder. Gabi saw him. He wanted to say something else, Gabi guessed, but he chickened out, whatever it was. She could almost see him thinking, wheels grinding ...

But he didn't say a peep.

It didn't matter much anymore. The crush on Max had been like a shooting star. Gabi saw it streaming across the sky, burning brightly, then fading quickly, like comets always do. He probably would have laughed out loud if he ever knew just how much of a crush Gabi had had on him just a few weeks earlier.

Thank goodness he never knew, Gabi thought.

Chapter 10

Bake No Mistake

Mom was brushing Gabi's hair. She'd end up just pulling it back anyway while painting, but that didn't matter. Gabi wanted to look good and feel good. It was, after all, her big day. And there was the chance that there might even be news reporters at school *again*.

Bakeover Part Two was here!

For weeks, it had been planned. First the sketches and then the approvals from all the members of student council and the PTA and the alumni as well. Gabi and Annie had worked to make sure the art project would go off without a hitch—and hopefully raise school spirit to new heights!

Genna stopped over to pick Gabi up so they could walk to school together. On the way they crossed the street and poked their heads into Daisy's Desserts. Genna couldn't contain herself. "Let's get some food!"

"Okay, but we'd better hurry," Gabi said. "I can't be late today!"

The girls walked up to the counter wearing big smiles on their faces.

"Well, hello, chickadees!" Babs cried. "Headed to school? Big day, we know!" Today she had her silver hair swept up into a knot. She started clapping. So did Dina. Pretty soon everyone in the bakery was clapping. It was a little embarrassing, but Gabi loved it. She was getting used to attention these days.

"Yes, the applause is for you!" Dina said.

Gabi felt her chest thump with pride. What other bakery serves up self-confidence with a side of sugar frosting? This was too much. But there was more.

"And of course, we are also proud because of …"

Dina pulled out a new menu from under the cash register. "Ta-da!"

A sample of the new menu! The new stock wasn't coming in for a week or so. Dina pointed out all of Gabi's art on it. It was so weird to see her drawings on something so official! It looked amazing!

Since Dina and Babs knew it was the big mural day, they'd packed boxes (and boxes!) of homemade donuts for all the kids who would be there to paint. What could Gabi say when she spotted the four big bags stuffed with boxes of treats? She threw her arms around each of them and held back the big wave of tears inside.

"They're all peanut free, and two boxes are gluten free too," Babs whispered. "Nothing but the best for our girls!"

"Hold on! Hold on!" cried a voice from the other side of the bakery. There was Daisy with a giant camera, snapping photos of them all. Genna mugged for the camera in each one, of course. Gabi was just counting her breaths so she wouldn't cry. The treats, the menu, the big day, everything. It was so much to take in!

"Thank you," she gushed to Daisy.

Daisy gently brushed a hair off Gabi's forehead. "You've got the killer outfit on, with the overalls and funky tie-dye tee, the high tops, the poncho. Wow. You figured it out after all, didn't you? Now promise me you'll report back on the mural—or will I see it on the evening news?" she teased.

Dina snapped a pick of Gabi, Genna, and Daisy. "Can I post this on my blog? Do you mind?" Daisy asked. "I want to share the new menu with every-one. And we can brag about your mural too. Get me a snapshot of that when it's completed."

It was a good photo. Gabi's hair was in a per-fect twist. Genna's smile was one thousand watts. Daisy's eyes glistened. They looked so happy and so connected. And finally Gabi was one-hundred percent *visible*!

Gabi thanked Daisy and the others once again, and they were off to school. The bags were sort of heavy, but school was only a few blocks away. Gabi and Genna lugged it all successfully and made it there before the first bell.

Principal Keystone and Annie were ready and waiting. He'd called a few connections to get donations: paint, paintbrushes, and aprons so kids didn't mess up their clothes. In the process of planning ways to bring more spirit to PS 33, it seemed as if Principal Keystone had caught as much school spirit as anyone. He stood there with a smile on his face and his paint smock on, ready to work.

Annie gave Gabi a high-five and said, "Let's do this!"

The students would be coming in shifts according to a schedule, class by class. They'd fill in portions of the mural pattern that Gabi, Annie, and their helpers had drawn on the wall the week before.

She was nervous. What if the pattern they'd created didn't work? What if it looked like garbage?

Or ... what if it had energy, momentum, and

power, just like she hoped? She let herself dare to dream that it would turn out perfectly.

From the moment the first student dipped his brush into a blue jar of paint, Gabi's fears vanished. Kids were taking this so seriously. They were paying attention to the details and working together in a way that you'd never guess kids who jostled in the hall and called each other crude names could. But they did!

Principal Keystone oversaw the process. He'd assigned different teachers to keep tabs on students too. And Gabi was there for all of it, answering questions, giving suggestions for paint colors, consulting with Annie when decisions needed to be made, darkening pencil sketch lines where they had smudged.

She felt just like Daisy, whirling around her bakery—present and needed and heard. And it was wonderful.

It took five hours and three-hundred and twelve students. By 2:37 that day, the mural was painted.

There, up on the wall, were Daisy's words, larger than life:

HAVE PATIENCE

TRY NEW THINGS

IMPOSSIBLE IS WHAT NO ONE ELSE HAS DONE

TAKE PRIDE

But it wasn't just written in big letters. When you looked closely, it became clear that each word was made of interconnected students—holding hands, leaning on each other, touching noses, high-fiving. And then, along the bottom of the mural, the words: *We are all connected at PS 33!*

Annie smiled at Gabi, and they bumped hips.

And then Genna gave Gabi the biggest hug ever when she saw the mural—especially when she saw two girls in the picture who she knew right away were Gabi and her. The two girls were connected by a book, which the Genna girl was writing in and the Gabi girl was drawing in, their pencils touching.

Photos were taken, the reporter came back, and during end-of-day announcements, Principal Keystone thanked Gabi and Annie over the loud-speaker. Everyone in the whole building began clapping from their classrooms, and it felt like a rumble of exciting thunder through the building.

The mural was there, forever a part of the school. And every kid at school had taken part. Gabi, Genna, Max, and even—especially—Annie. They were all part of one big community.

Mission accomplished.

Business at Daisy's Desserts continued to be a big success too. Visitors marveled at the array of baked goods—including all the new and improved gluten-free and nut-free and other allergen-free offerings.

Gabi continued to go to Daisy's after school to finish up her homework and just hang out. Genna joined her too, when she had time. But Genna had gotten much busier these days working on her own stuff. She said that listening to Daisy and watching Gabi's transformation had inspired her to have a transformation of her own. So she enrolled in a comedy improvisation class way downtown in the city.

"If I'm going to be a comedy writer of bad jokes and puns then I better learn to tell them the right way," Genna said.

One afternoon, while Gabi was seated by herself at a small table by the window, doodling in crayon on the white table cover as always, she had a visitor.

"Can I sit here?"

It was Max.

Gabi had seen him here and there at school, but they hadn't talked since the day of the mural. Part of that was due to the fact that Max was often hanging out with the noisy group of kids that Gabi didn't really like so much. But, to be honest, she wasn't sure how true that was anymore. The girls Gabi referred to as the "meanies" weren't actually all that mean, except for that one day in assembly so many weeks ago.

And even Annie herself had turned out to be not so bad. Could it be that Gabi just wasn't taking silly comments and snarky looks as personally now as she used to? And could it be that she just took them all too personally in the first place? She couldn't be sure.

"How have you been?" Max asked.

"Fine. You?"

"Fine."

"So, what's new?" Gabi asked.

"Not much."

"How's school?"

"Fine," Max replied.

"So ..."

There were long pauses between questions. Gabi felt like she was the one driving the conversation for a change, while Max looked like he was the one who felt awkward. What was up with him?

After a while, Max reached down into his book

bag. "I have something of yours that I've been meaning to give back to you for the longest time," he said.

"You do?" Gabi asked, surprised.

"Yeah, I'm sorry. I've carried this with me every day, trying to find the right time to give it back to you ..."

"Give it *back*?" Gabi hadn't a clue about what he was talking about.

Max pulled out a piece of paper folded into smaller squares. Gabi knew what it was before he even opened it. She recognized her paper, her artwork ... her confession about her secret crush.

It was the portrait of Max that Gabi had sketched weeks before. It was wrinkled and smudged. But it was clearly Max.

"You drew me."

"Yeah," Gabi said cautiously. She felt her chest clench. "I never meant for you to see that."

"I think you were running out of the bakeshop and you dropped it. That day with the hot chocolate?"

Ugh, so Max had witnessed that after all.

"I helped Daisy clean up, and we found this. I told her I'd return it to you ... but I never quite got around to it."

Gabi decided that in this moment, the best thing to say was as little as possible. She was too caught off guard, too embarrassed, too completely over-whelmed to do much more than that.

"You want it back?" Max finally asked.

Gabi shook her head. "You can keep it, if you want."

"Yeah, uh ... okay. Thanks." Max said. "Hey, I brought my homework too. Can you go over those science lab questions with me?"

Gabi nodded. "Of course. But won't your friends miss you?" She looked toward his crew at the other table, laughing loudly and splitting a huge piece of chocolate cake.

"Nah, they all know I've been working up the courage to come talk to you," he said with a grin.

From behind the two of them, Daisy swooped

in with two small mugs of mocha cocoa whipped cream delight. Something fancy like that. They were sprinkled with flakes of chocolate. She also had a sampling of cookie bites, all allergy-friendly, of course.

"On the house," Daisy winked.

Back to the Blog

Home

Meet the Bakers

Recipes

- Cakes
- Cookies
- Tray Bakes
- Breads
- Gluten Free
- Vegan
- Dairy Free
- Other

Archive

- January
- February
- March

Hello, my sweets!

What a month it has been! You may have had the pleasure of seeing my good friend and neighbor Gabriela on the local news. She has worked on a few wonderful art projects at her school and at the bakery. She drew amazing spot illustrations for my new menu, including the coolest little kick-line of pies you've ever seen.

And coming soon: I will be offering a daily *savory* pie in the shop. In fact, we are moving to include more meat and vegetable treats, baked up just for our sugar-free friends!

Thanks to my pal Gabriela, I have been working to produce a fuller inventory of gluten-free and nut-free items. We are always trying to meet the needs of our neighborhood and friends.

Until the flowers bloom this spring, stop into the shop for colorful goodies to help kick winter to the curb! And there'll be plenty of challah for Passover, loads of hot cross buns for Easter bunnies, and much, much more.

The door is always open for new ideas at Daisy's! Stop by to say hi and tell us how we can better serve you!

xo, Daisy

From the *Kitchen* of *Daisy Duncan*

Gabi's Nut-free Krispy Bites

Crunchy and chewy, this simple version of Gabi's Krispy Treats is tasty—and safe if you have a tree-nut or peanut allergy.

Ingredients:

1 package of mini-marshmallows (about 40)

3 tablespoons butter

Microwave-safe bowl

1 box of puffed rice cereal (about 6 cups)

Parchment paper

1 large baking pan

1 package of chocolate kisses (nut-free)

Directions:

1. Place marshmallows and butter in microwave-safe bowl. Microwave for 2 minutes and stir. Microwave for additional minute.

2. Pour puffed rice cereal into bowl with melted marshmallow mixture. Mix completely.

3. Place parchment paper inside pan.

4. Pour mixture into pan and press down to fill evenly. Cut into squares.

5. Optional: melt chocolate kisses in microwave-safe bowl. Dip edge of each square into the chocolate and cool to harden chocolate.

About the Bakers

Daisy

Owner of Daisy's Desserts! With a frizzy head of magical red hair, sunny disposition, and a treasure trove of recipes passed down from her dear Nana Belle, this always-optimistic baker is ready to serve you! Along with her zany baking team—Dina, Babs, and Carlos—Daisy aims to transform our city neighborhood with sugar, spice, and everything nice. From custards to cupcakes, Daisy always seems to have the recipe for "baked love" up her flour-dusted sleeve. Inside Daisy's Desserts, the impossible somehow becomes frosted with possibility!

Dina

Baker and waitress Dina specializes in sweets, especially when it comes to her personality! Designated mother hen of the crew, Dina not only has a way with a rolling pin and a whisk but also with our customers! She is always suggesting new recipes and encouraging Daisy to try new ingredients from around the globe.

Carlos

Daisy's number-one confidante and trusted sidekick in the kitchen, Carlos has a twinkle in his eye and pep in his step. A family man with four sweet-toothed kids at home, Carlos is always inventing and testing new recipes in the kitchen of Daisy's Desserts. He is the master mix-man—to date, he's invented cookies, cakes, and even Daisy's line of sweet treats for dogs. His favorite saying is, "I keep experimenting until I find the right formula!"

Babs

Like a Hollywood starlet from another era, Babs is always dressed to impress with a bouffant do and an apron to match every shade of lipstick. Our wisecracking baking beauty has a lingo all her own, calling customers "peach" or "sugar" before sneaking them samples of Daisy's latest baked goodies. Babs is also our bakery's guardian angel—years ago, she was BFFs with Daisy's Nana Belle.

Talk it out with Daisy!

Different is great! But different can also be challenging. Just ask Gabi!

Think about something that makes you seem different from others. How does it make you feel?

Can you think of ways that differences make us stronger or make us unique?

Was there ever a time that being different helped make you a leader?

Good friends can help you through life's challenges. Come up with some examples in the story where you see evidence of good friendships. Then think of a time in your life when you were a good friend or someone was a good friend to you.

Laura Dower

About the Author

Laura Dower worked in marketing and editorial in children's publishing for many years before taking a big leap to the job of full-time author. She has published more than 100 kids' books including the popular tween series From the Files of Madison Finn. A longtime Girl Scout leader, Cub Scout leader, and swim mom, Laura lives with her family in New York.

Lilly Lazuli

About the Illustrator

London based illustrator Lilly Lazuli has a penchant for all things colorful and sweet! Originally from Hawaii, Lilly creates artwork that has a bright and cheerful aesthetic. She gains most of her inspiration from traveling, vintage fashion, and ogling beautiful cakes. She enjoys making eye-catching artwork that makes people smile.

the Dessert Diaries

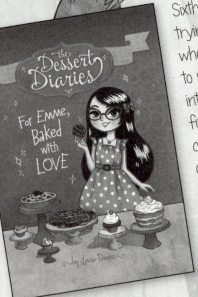

Friendship is the best recipe!

Sixth-grader Emme is always trying to keep the peace. But when her parents decide to split, and her BFFs get into a major fight, Emme finds herself caught in the crossfire. Can the opening of a new bakery help Emme find peace again?

Starting at a new school in sixth grade isn't easy. And the reason Maggie's at a new school is even worse. On top of it all, Maggie's little sister is driving her crazy! But when Maggie stumbles upon a unique bakery in her new neighborhood, life starts getting a little sweeter.

Sixth-grade science whiz Kiki loves to experiment in the science lab, so she jumps at the chance to experiment in the kitchen with the bakers at Daisy's Desserts. But when a super-sized bakery threatens to close Daisy's down, can Kiki use her smarts to help find a solution?

For MORE GREAT BOOKS go to

www.mycapstone.com